BEYOND WESPIRTECH

SHORT FICTION FROM THE ENTANGLED UNIVERSE

MARY E. LOWD

CONTENTS

PREFACE

I began writing seriously right after college. For the first time in my life, as far as I could remember, my year was no longer shaped by the academic calendar, my day no longer ruled by a class schedule. It was glorious. I was lost. The only landmarks were ones I chose for myself—imaginary deadlines for writing stories that no one had asked me to write.

During this time, I was living in Seattle with my spouse as he pursued a PhD in computer science at the University of Washington. His life still had a shape I recognized, but mine had gone all amorphous. I spent my days walking my dog, an orange Sheltie, around Green Lake, talking to him about the stories I was trying to write. It was a devastatingly lonely time. Most of my life has involved some degree of loneliness, as there are very few places I seem to belong, and I struggle to get along with most people. But those early years in Seattle involved a special, extreme degree of isolation. My spouse was busy, and the internet hadn't fully bloomed yet, so it was harder to connect with people online than it is now.

Most of my fictional universe centered on an imaginary science institute—Wespirtech—inspired by the intense experience, both good and bad, I'd had attending the tech college where I met my spouse. He was still part of that world, in a way, having moved from undergraduate to graduate studies. I went with him to department functions and some grad student parties, but I was always an outsider. The spouse. Not really part of it.

The stories in this collection capture that feeling of being just outside of the bright, shining center of the universe where all the exciting things are happening. You can still see them. They still affect you. But your life has recentered somewhere else, somewhere on the fringes of the universe.

When you create a big enough universe, there's still excitement, even out on the edges. So, if you've ever felt like you don't quite fit into the middle, where everything is happening, but you'd still like to be involved, join me here—beyond Wespirtech.

NOTE ON THE 2ND EDITION

This book was originally released in 2014 before I had really finished writing it. My first two novels—*Otters In Space* and *Otters In Space 2: Jupiter, Deadly*—had recently been picked up by a small publisher, FurPlanet, and I wanted to sell copies at local events. However, a table with only two books on it is a sad affair. So, I took all the short stories I'd written at the time and managed to put together three meagre collections—*Welcome to Wespirtech*, *Beyond Wespirtech*, and *The Opposite of Memory*—which I self-published. For the next nine years, I pursued traditional publishing, and my self-published collections fell to the side. But now that I'm in my forties and tired of the nonsense inherent to the publishing industry, I've returned to my roots, and it was time to make this book what it was always meant to be.

Four of the stories in this book were written after the first edition was released, and two of those stories are wholly original to this edition, never published before.

I never stopped loving this book, even when it was incomplete. Now that I see what it's become, I love it even more. I hope, dear reader, you will love it too.

1

———

REKINDLE THE SUN

The yellow sun of Heffe VIII beamed onto Kerri's face through the freighter ship's window. She'd been watching intently through the window ever since the ship entered the Heffen solar system. "It's hard to believe that's a dying sun," Kerri said. It was still so bright and dazzling, hanging in the black, velvet sky. It looked young and promising, not old and fading. Kerri turned to her husband, Alan, who was sitting beside her, and smiled. "It'll be good to finally see Heffe," she said.

Alan, with the winningly mischievous smile that first captured Kerri's attention, began speaking to her in Heffen. Kerri recognized the language; Alan had been learning it for months, ever since he'd been hired for this job. He had a knack for languages that Kerri knew she didn't have. When he finished, he said, "That was a Heffen love poem for you. I found it in one of my books."

Kerri was touched. She wondered what, exactly, the poem meant, but she didn't ask. Already worried about coming to live on a world where she didn't speak the native language, she found comfort in pretending not to mind. Kerri and Alan sat quietly for the rest of the flight across the Heffen system. Kerri wished she were better with languages.

As the ship landed, Alan said, "You know, this flight, the whole way from Wespirtech, will only take a few minutes when Anna finishes her elasti-drive."

Kerri heard about Anna Karlingoff a lot. She was one of Alan's colleagues at Wespirtech, one of the other physicists. When Alan first started talking about Anna, Kerri was inclined to be jealous. Alan teased her about it. After a while, Kerri asked around, and it turned out that Anna was madly in love with a geneticist. She was no threat, and Kerri felt foolish for doubting Alan.

Now that Alan had left Wespirtech for good, Kerri realized she would miss hearing about Anna. Living on Heffe would be better than her years with Alan at Wespirtech had been. Here, she could learn about the culture and make friends of her own instead of just hearing about his. At Wespirtech, she had been one of very few spouses, and the scientists kept mostly to each other. The Western Spiral Arm Planetary Institute of Technology, better known as Wespirtech, was the foremost outpost of scientific and technological advancement in the known universe, but it wasn't a very friendly place to live for an outsider. She could not be more of an outsider on Heffe VIII than she had been there.

On Heffe VIII, there would be cities and gardens, museums, concerts, and shops. Kerri would have her own home. She could grow a garden again... It had been too many years since she'd had a real garden. At Wespirtech, the best she could manage was a few potted plants. Yes, Heffe VIII would be much better than the cold, steel buildings of Wespirtech, surrounded by that desolate moon.

Finally, the freighter ship, which had landed many minutes before, finished its complicated decontamination and hatch unlocking procedures. Kerri and Alan were free to disembark.

Their bags were already packed, and their quarters on the ship were returned to the friendly but sterile state they'd known when Kerri and Alan boarded months ago. It looked like a hotel room, replete with generic, floral paintings and bad lighting. Kerri was glad she wouldn't be living there any longer. Even their rooms at Wespirtech had been better.

The little, yellow sun blazed, almost mockingly, as Kerri and Alan stepped, holding hands, onto the world that was to be their new home. Alan looked at the sun appreciatively, like a mathematician looking at a particularly complicated and elegant differential equation. Up to the next twenty years of his life would be spent trying to save that dying sun. Kerri squeezed his hand proudly.

The Petriezskian Democracy had sent a welcoming squadron, and Alan, their new fusion dynamics specialist, was greeted with honors. For Kerri, it was exciting but unsettling. A full squadron of stiffly uniformed officials, with flags from each of the Heffen nations waving above their heads, had come to greet her! Except...they weren't there for her, really. They were there to greet Alan, and Kerri was just the wife. She felt out of place.

Still, it was very interesting. Kerri had never seen a live Heffen before, much less shaken hands with one, although she had been studying all their records and had seen many 2Ds and a few holoscans. While Alan spoke in Heffen with the head of the welcoming party and was introduced to a series of new colleagues, Kerri looked closely at the faces of this alien race, her new neighbors.

By far, most of the Heffen present were Petriezski. That was not surprising, since theirs was the nation Kerri and Alan landed in and were soon to live in. The Petriezski had the richest and most politically powerful government on Heffe VIII, and, therefore, had been the ones to commission Alan.

Scanning over the crowd, Kerri picked out one face that was

not Petriezskian. The flat-faced and short-furred Golan stood out quite a bit in the crowd of Petriezski with their longer, more articulated faces, and flowing fur. Of course, the red and gold ribbons draped over his shoulders, hanging almost to his feet, helped him stand out too. The Petriezski looked more formal and dignified. They were really quite handsome, the Petriezski were, with their ruffs of fur flowing out of the collars and over the shoulders of their uniforms. The Golan individual looked funnier with his stout, square frame and short fur. Kerri imagined he was a much more colorful individual...or maybe it was just those ribbons.

Kerri took Alan's arm and gave it a steady squeeze. *I'm tired and ready to go* that squeeze said. Alan looked flustered but took the hint. The formalities were soon wrapped up. Kerri and Alan were shown to a hoverpod and flown to their new home.

ALAN ORDERED the *karfanor* special for two, a Petriezskian dish. Kerri knew he tended to order dishes that were too bland for her, but she still couldn't read the menu, and objecting would have been too hard. Besides, it was sweet the way he made romantic gestures, like ordering the meal for two.

They were at the fanciest restaurant in Ques'trian, the capital city of the Petriezski Nation, and the city to which they lived closest. Still, it was a twenty-minute drive by hoverpod away. It had been a few months since Kerri and Alan arrived on Heffe, although Kerri felt like she was still settling in. Alan had begun his work in earnest a while ago, studying the sun, trying to select the best plan of attack. Tonight's dinner was a celebration. He'd located a similar but unwanted sun in a nearby star system and planned to mine it for matter transfusions to pump into the Heffen sun. He had high hopes for the plan working and was in high spirits. Kerri was happy to see him happy.

"The Petriezski are preparing a ship for the mining expedition already," Alan said. "If you don't mind, I was planning to fly along with them. It would be a few months."

Alan was looking down as he said it, so he missed Kerri's momentary expression. By the time he looked up, expecting an answer, Kerri had recovered herself and managed to say, "Of course, if that would be best for your work, it'll be fine. It will give me time to work on my garden." Just at that moment, Kerri couldn't imagine doing much more than work on her garden without Alan there. She hadn't been into Ques'trian alone yet and was afraid of how she'd get by not knowing the language.

"How is your garden, Kerri?" he asked. "When will those plants you're having shipped from Earth X come?"

Kerri, happy to talk about her garden, reminded Alan of when the shipment would come and told him about all the different plants she'd ordered, including her special order for a kitty-willow tree, a favorite plant from her childhood. Then, she suggested that, maybe, before he left he could go with her to one of the local greenhouses and help her buy some native plants. It would let her get to work sooner, before the Earth X shipment came.

"I don't think there'll be time..." he said. "I'm sorry." Then, returning to his favorite solution, Alan muttered something about trying again to get Kerri a Keat. Kerri knew better than to pin her hopes on it.

For a while, when Kerri and Alan first arrived, Alan talked a lot about contacting Anna, pulling some strings, and seeing if he could get a hold of a Keat. Normally, Keats, a genetically advanced breed of parrot designed to act as translators, were reserved for important diplomats. However, Anna was dating the geneticist who designed them. Somehow though, Alan's promise never came through, and eventually he stopped mentioning it. From the gossip Kerri could gather through her limited correspondence over subspace, she suspected Alan's failure to procure a Keat through Anna had to do with her nasty breakup with the geneticist. She also suspected that Alan didn't know about it.

The *karfanor* special for two came, and Kerri and Alan were occupied for some time with eating. Kerri discovered she'd been right: Alan had ordered a meal too bland for her. It was all right though, and Alan seemed to like it. What Kerri wondered about was Golan food. She'd passed by a Golan kiosk on the street, teeming with the smell of exotic spices. It'd be too much for Alan. Maybe while Alan was gone on his mining expedition, she'd finally try it.

THE SHIPMENT of plants from Earth X, including Kerri's eagerly awaited kitty-willow tree, arrived while Alan was still gone. Kerri received notice of the arrival at home but would have to go into town in the hoverpod to pick the shipment up. She'd gone into town a few times already. Exploring the countryside, readying her garden for the coming shipment, and relaxing at home were good ways to spend time, but Kerri grew hungry for even the sight other people as the weeks without Alan stretched on. Eventually, she'd overcome her fears of a city where she stood out, the only human, and knew none of the language.

Fortunately, visiting Ques'trian alone had turned out to be very exciting. For one, the hoverpod was fun to drive, and while Alan was around he was always the one to handle the controls. During the long years at Wespirtech, Kerri had forgotten how much she loved flying hoverpods. At Wespirtech, there'd been no need for them, or for anything of their sort, since the entire institute was insulated in its steel and granite buildings with almost no access to the actual surface of the moon. There was nowhere to go that couldn't be reached by hallways and elevators.

Coming to Ques'trian to pick up her shipment from Earth X, Kerri zipped the hoverpod at an almost unsafe speed along the familiar path. She parked it near the capitol building in a particularly reputable hoverpod parking depot. Then, Kerri walked to the greenhouse that received her shipment, by way of her favorite Golan food kiosk. To begin with, ordering at the kiosk had involved a lot of complicated pointing and gesturing. By now, though, the Golan woman who ran the kiosk knew what Kerri would want, and the transaction was much simpler. Kerri placed the paper wrapped, spicy flavored, meat and pastry confection in her jacket pocket. She would eat it on her way back home.

Kerri felt alive when she got home and started unpacking her new plants. Some of them were merely bags of seeds or bunches of bulbs, waiting to be planted. A few of the plants, though, had been sent fully-grown. The most exciting of them was her kitty-willow tree. Kerri removed the tiny sapling from its box gingerly and carefully unwound the moistened cloth from its young roots.

The tree didn't look like much, just a branched stick at that particular moment. Kerri wished Alan were there with her to see and appreciate the unremarkable state of this thing that in less than a year would yield such amazing fruit, if fruit were an appropriate word. Kerri sighed. She felt the warmth of the sun on her back, and she imagined Alan out there, beyond the blue of the sky, finding more warmth to bring to the sun. He was working, so she would work too. If she worked hard, she might be able to get her plants in the ground and growing in time for the Heffen spring, only a few months away. Perhaps, when Alan came home, she could surprise him with a garden already in full bloom.

KERRI HAD GROWN USED to visiting Ques'trian and walking among the Heffen, but she was nervous about tonight: in a matter of hours, she would be faced with her first Heffen guests. Alan offered to pick up *klaufon* pies in the city. He didn't want to inconvenience Kerri with preparing a meal for his colleagues who were coming over to discuss work. *Klaufon* pies from the city would be all ready except for baking and sure to please. Alan hadn't met a Heffen yet who didn't like *klaufon* pie. Kerri knew it would have been easier. She was glad Alan had offered, and part of her hated herself for turning him down. Yet, by the time Alan's colleagues were expected Kerri felt proud of her choice. The combination of Petriezskian and her own dishes, all made with fruits and vegetables from her own garden, made a delightful spread. The table looked beautiful.

The guests, when they arrived, turned out to be three Petriezski men, a Petriezski woman, and one Golan, also a man. Kerri could tell one of the Petriezski was a woman by the black touches of fur in her ruff. The color of Petriezski fur varied widely among shades of orange, red, gold, tan, and brown. And, almost all Petriezski had white markings on their long, thin faces and their ruffs. However, only the women had black shadings as well. The Petriezski woman, Kerri decided, was a particularly beautiful Heffen.

Golan men and women were harder for Kerri to tell apart. She could tell that Alan's Golan guest was a man mainly from his bearing. Other than that, he was a funny, rounded, little fellow with a face flattened into folds like almost all the other Golan she'd seen. His main discerning feature was a strangely familiar braid of red and gold ribbons draped over his shoulders. Kerri remembered seeing him before, but couldn't quite place him.

After a few minutes of talking, Alan turned to Kerri and

asked, "Is the table ready? Can I ask them to come, sit down, and eat?"

Kerri replied, quietly to Alan, that everything was ready before the guests arrived, and turned to lead them all to the table. As they walked, Kerri realized why the gold and red ribbons were familiar. This Golan visitor must have been the same as the first Golan she'd ever seen, the one in the crowd when she and Alan landed on Heffe VIII. Kerri wondered idly what the ribbons were for and why she hadn't seen other Heffen, or at least other Golan, wearing them.

Once in the dining room and settled into eating, the Heffen guests all seemed pleased by the dinner Kerri had prepared for them. Kerri smiled whenever one of them seemed to be giving her a compliment. She still didn't understand Heffen but had come a long way towards understanding Heffen body language from her trips into Ques'trian on her own.

During the meal, Kerri noticed that the Golan kept mainly to her dishes, avoiding the standard Petriezskian dishes she'd made. The Petriezski behaved quite oppositely. Kerri was flattered that they all seemed happy with the meal, but she was particularly pleased by the Golan's behavior. Kerri felt a greater affinity for the Golan already, simply because she preferred Golan food, always eating at the Golan kiosks when she went to town alone. Also, this Golan laughed more than his colleagues, and he seemed less interested in the conversation. He kept looking at her, as if they shared a secret, although she couldn't imagine what it could be.

When the meal was over, Alan led the Heffen away from the dining room to begin discussing their latest results with the sun. Kerri stayed in the kitchen and dining room, clearing the table up. She could hear them talking in the living room, and she knew what they were talking about. The matter transfusions to the sun had not gone quite as expected, and Alan was working on a new plan. There were still hopes, though, that the irregularities in his scans would settle out over time and the sun would stabilize again, but as a much younger sun with a longer life ahead of it.

Kerri found herself wondering what would happen if the scan results did stabilize. If the sun were suddenly saved and Alan no longer needed here, would they move away? She liked the idea of returning to a world of humans, a world where she spoke the language. And yet... She loved the Heffen countryside. The trees of Heffe VIII were not quite like trees she'd seen anywhere else. They were lither, more arching. Sometimes their branches grew like corkscrews, twisting entirely around. The forests were certainly something to see.

Lost in her reveries, Kerri was surprised to see the Golan man return from the living room on his own. "Do you want something?" she asked, reflexively, forgetting he probably wouldn't understand. She grabbed a glass from the cupboard and held it out, offering it to him, hoping he'd understand it as an offer to get him something to drink.

"You don't speak Heffen, do you?" the Golan asked.

Recovering from the surprise, Kerri discovered herself facing a situation she had honestly never expected to face: since Kerri had slowly come to believe she'd never manage to learn Heffen, she never expected to have a conversation with one of them.

Before Kerri recovered enough to answer, the Golan added the question: "You do speak your own language, don't you? Or is my English that bad?"

"I'm sorry," Kerri answered. "I was just so surprised...I didn't know any of you spoke English."

The Golan laughed. "The others don't," he said. "They're not used to learning languages because they were brought up here," the Golan gestured expansively around.

Kerri looked confused, so the Golan clarified, saying "The

Petriezski language is the most common language on our planet, but it's not the only one."

"I didn't realize..." Kerri said.

"You probably think of it as 'Heffen' don't, you? That's all right. They do too," he added, gesturing back towards the room where Alan was talking to his compatriots. "My name is Baury," he added. "You probably didn't catch that when we came in." Kerri blushed at the reference to her verbal illiteracy of Heffen. "Why doesn't Alan translate for you?" Baury asked innocently, not seeing Kerri's embarrassment. "I'm sure you wouldn't be interested in everything we have to say, but you probably would have enjoyed some of the compliments."

Kerri smiled and said, "I could tell the compliments."

"Yes, but you don't know what they meant," Baury teased with a chuckle.

Kerri, warming to the first face to face conversation she'd had with anyone other than Alan in almost a year, countered back, "Then why don't you tell me?"

"Aah," Baury smiled, for his face seemed built into a smile, "you'll have to ask Alan."

Kerri felt oddly rebuffed by Baury's comment. As Baury probably guessed, she was curious about the compliments. What he didn't know was that Kerri wouldn't ask Alan. She knew his mind was too busied with his work to remember such minor details, comments made to his wife rather than to him. "Why are you out here?" Kerri asked, feeling prickly, "shouldn't you be in there, talking with them about saving your *dying* sun?"

"I'm not a scientist," Baury shrugged. "I work with them, but I'm mainly here because of Trenti, the tallest Petriezski out there. He's my brother in law, married my one and only sister. He sees that I get invited along." Baury looked up and grinned a particularly jovial grin. "They're going to have a litter soon, you know. I hope they're all beautiful, little pug-faced babies that look just like her." Baury paused before continuing, "My sister's beautiful," he said. "She's why I moved here...if it weren't for her, I would never have left Gola."

Affected by Baury's warmth and the loyalty towards his sister evident in his tone, Kerri warmed to him again. She invited him to follow her out to her garden, where she had a few plants that needed her tending every evening. As Kerri clipped the browning buds on her cameline night bloomers, Baury told her about his beloved homeland, the nation of Gola.

From then on, whenever Alan's colleagues visited, Baury came along. He played the part of heckler in their scientific conversations, but mostly he would separate from the rest and talk to Kerri. He told her that if he must speak in a foreign tongue to talk to friends, he might as well exercise his newest one, and Kerri was the only person to whom he could speak in English (since Alan avoided it in favor of the Petriezski tongue). Kerri welcomed the company and enjoyed learning about the political situation on Heffe VIII. Alan never mentioned it, but he was glad to see Kerri making a friend. Although Baury was the Heffen who made the least sense to him of all his colleagues, if Kerri liked him, Alan was glad of it.

SPRING CAME, and Kerri's kitty-willow tree finally bloomed. The flowers were simple, five-petaled, pink blossoms. The tree was still small, only about two feet tall, but it was beginning to look more like a tree and less like a twig. The extra year of growth before blooming, for it had failed to bloom at all during its first spring on Heffe VIII, had done well for it. Kerri showed it proudly to both her husband and her new friend; neither was particularly appreciative, but neither understood what was coming.

Days passed and Kerri expectantly watched the blossoms

lose their petals and grow into fuzzy buds. She checked on her tree daily. Placed prominently in the center of her garden, it was the first plant she tended in the morning and the last she saw to at night. Therefore, it was hardly surprising that she should be there when the first of the downy, gray buds uncurled and dropped onto the soil beneath its parent tree.

Kerri reached down and picked up the tiny, perfectly formed kitten that was the seed of her kitty-willow tree. She smiled at the tiny cat as it explored the palm of her hand. Yet, Kerri couldn't help but notice the difference between her current happiness and the sheer elation she remembered feeling whenever her kitty-willow tree bloomed during her childhood. *The senses dull as you age,* she thought. *Nonetheless, it feels good to remember the joys from childhood.*

Over the course of the following month, the rest of the kitty-willow seeds uncurled and fell from their natal branches. Each kitten-seed lived only a week or so, just enough time to travel and explore, searching for a good place to die, leaving its body to grow into a new kitty-willow tree. Kerri, unsure what their effect would be on the local, Heffen ecological balance, gathered all the kitten-seeds up and made sure none escaped from her own garden.

Alan, although he'd been told to expect the kitty-willow's blooming, didn't notice the box of kitten-seeds Kerri kept and played with all month long, nor did he think to ask after the tree. Kerri chose not to force them on his attention, since he was very busy with his studies. The sun's reaction to the matter transfusions had finally stabilized, but the sun was still dying. Alan spent all his time at his work, trying to formulate a new plan to revitalize the sun. Kerri didn't want to disturb him. Her kitty-willow tree would bloom again next year.

～

"SOMEDAY, I'd like to meet your sister," Kerri told Baury, as he helped her clean up from another of Alan's dinner parties.

"Aah," Baury sighed. "My sister doesn't leave home much. She feels too much like an outsider here, and she's kept very busy with the little ones, you know. Also, Trenti doesn't like guests in their house much, so I'm afraid you probably won't get the chance." Baury smiled conciliatorily. "She doesn't speak English, anyway," he said.

Kerri tried to imagine what life must be like for Baury's sister, living in a foreign country. Kerri imagined it must be lonely, much like her own loneliness. "It must be hard for her," Kerri said. "Aren't there other Golan she spends time with? I see Golan men and women when I'm in the city."

"You see them running the kiosks," Baury said. "Am I right?"

Kerri realized that Baury was right, she never saw Golan anywhere other than running the kiosks. She nodded acquiescence.

"There are very few of us here, and we all feel it," Baury said. "In fact, I'm the only Golan I know who's brave enough to wear these," Baury added fingering the red and gold braid ribbons that were, as always, draped over his shoulders.

"I've often wondered what those are..." Kerri said.

Baury chuckled. "Striking aren't they? They're a religious talisman. But the Petriezski don't believe in our religion. So, most of my fellow countrymen keep their faith quieter than I keep mine." Baury winked at her, and said, "I've never much cared for keeping a low profile."

The friends finished clearing up the kitchen and dining room, and after Baury checked to see that the science talk was still in full force, the two of them retired to a bench in Kerri's garden. It was a warm night, despite the cooling of the world's sun, and distant stars twinkled in the sky above them.

"Why don't the other Golan wear talismans?" Kerri asked. "They stand out anyway...you can't help that..."

"You mean our flat faces, square bodies, and short fur," Baury said. "Yes, you're right, we can't hide that we look different. But, we can hide that we *are* different. Some Golan think they get treated better if they pretend to be Petriezski who were just born in the wrong country. I don't know. Maybe they do get treated better," Baury ended pensively.

Kerri shared in the silence for a minute, and then asked, "Do they treat you badly, Baury?"

Baury, who was not the type to stay sad for long, smiled his characteristic smile and said, "Not to my flat face," he said, and, then, nudging her in the arm, "there's no telling what they say behind my back. Actually," he said, bucking up even more, "you can hear what they say behind my back. Listen for the phrase '*Galountan Golan*.' They might say it in front of you...although, please don't tell me if they do."

Kerri began to speak, looking as if she might ask a question, but Baury interrupted her before she could form it. "I won't tell you what the phrase means," he said. "It's very offensive, and I don't even want the idea in your pretty head."

Kerri bowed her pretty head in submission. She didn't mind not knowing.

"Now," Baury continued, full of bluster, "our name for them is much less insulting. Roughly translated, let's see, I believe it would be something like '*needle-nose*.'"

Kerri laughed at the accuracy of the image, and Baury laughed with her. They both felt good, laughing together, and they were still laughing when Baury's brother-in-law Trenti came bursting out into the garden to find them. An animated conversation between the brothers-in-law pursued. Kerri judged from Trenti's gestures and body language that he wanted Baury to come with him, but Baury shook his head and remained resolute. Trenti, agitated and clearly still excited by whatever news had brought him out to them, waved his arm dismissively, as if to say: fine, stay here if you must. Then, he hurried away.

Wide-eyed, Kerri asked, "What was that all about?"

"Oh, big news. Big breakthrough," Baury said, with much less animation than Trenti'd had. "Something about tightening the atoms in the sun up. You should ask Alan. I'm sure he understands it better than I do."

Kerri noted to herself that understanding a subject better didn't necessarily mean one could explain a subject better. Nonetheless, she decided not to press the matter. She would wait until their guests left for the evening and learn about the breakthrough from Alan. Fortunately for the state of her curiosity, Trenti returned soon to tell Baury they were leaving.

Right before Baury left to join the others, he remembered a piece of information he'd heard that he thought would interest Kerri. He told her he'd heard of another human moving to Heffe, and he'd heard she was living nearby. Perhaps, Kerri should look this human woman up? She might, he suggested, be as lonely for human friendship as Kerri.

Kerri saw Baury to the door, where he rejoined his Petriezski friends. The colleagues bid goodbye to Alan in Heffen, and Baury smiled a knowing goodbye to Kerri. The door shut, and Kerri turned towards Alan, only to find herself swept up in his arms. Alan lifted Kerri in the air and spun around. "We have a new plan!" he said joyfully.

Kerri broke into a grin at the sight of his grin. She hadn't realized how hard it must have been for him that the last plan didn't work. The spinning ended, and Kerri, as soon as her feet returned to the floor, hugged Alan close. "I'm so glad," she said. Then, pulling back enough to look him in the face, she added, "Do tell me about it?"

"It's the strong force," Alan explained. "It's a number, and that number's the same all over the universe. That number, the value of the strong force, partly determines how atoms are built...the way their nuclei hold together... We're going to make it bigger...that will make the force stronger...but only locally."

Kerri looked at her husband, soaking up his excitement, happy but confused. Alan picked up on the confusion and added, "If we make the strong force stronger, just in the vicinity of their sun, then the atoms of the sun will pull closer together, heating up the fusion. Combined with the matter transfusions we've already given it..." Alan drew a deep breath, "...it just might do the trick."

"That makes sense," Kerri said, appeasing her husband's need for her to understand. And, though Kerri wasn't sure she understood, it did sound reasonable to her. She'd taken physics classes, but it was many years back, and by now the concepts sounded, at best, familiar to her.

"I should be working on it," Alan said, looking distracted by his physics thoughts. "There's so much to be done."

Before Alan drifted away from her entirely, back into his world of abstracts, Kerri re-caught his attention and asked, "Have you heard anything about another human moving to Heffe?" She looked at Alan expectantly, hoping for a useful answer. When Alan merely looked baffled and started to shake his head, Kerri gave up the hope. "Baury mentioned something about it..." Kerri mumbled.

"Actually," Alan said after another few moments, "that does sound familiar. She's a widow, I think, with a little daughter. Some kind of botanist... horticulturalist... gardener... something..." Alan trailed off, but then his face brightened, and he said, "Maybe you two would hit off. You should look her up." And with that, Alan was back to his work.

KERRI PARKED her hoverpod within sight of the widow's estate, then got out to walk. The estate stood in an open valley, a small house, with a large wall growing out behind it. The wall was stone and fenced in a sizeable area behind the house. The widow must, Kerri thought, have come to Heffe VIII with quite a fortune to be able to buy herself such an estate. Or maybe she'd been commissioned by the Petriezski government like Alan had?

Kerri approached the house from the side, taking the chance to jump up and look over the rock wall. Inside the wall lay a simple yard, children's toys strewn about on short grass. Kerri was disappointed. If the widow was a gardener, she didn't have much of a garden. Kerri followed the wall to the house, and as she came closer, another structure came into sight, formerly hidden behind the house. This second building had glass walls and glowed with an orange light from inside. Kerri perked up at the sight. Perhaps the widow was a gardener after all, for who else would have a greenhouse?

Standing at the front door, preparing to knock, Kerri heard giggling come from nearby. She looked down to see a small girl, perhaps four or five, hiding under the draping branches and red leaves of an ornamental maple tree. The little girl's eyes widened, and her mouth formed the shape of an 'O'. "You saw me!" she said. "I was going to surprise you."

"You did surprise me," Kerri said. "I'm not used to trees that talk to me."

The little girl laughed. "I'm not a tree! Can't you see me?"

Kerri played along and said, "Oh! You're the little girl inside the tree...I didn't see you before. Is your mother home?"

"You saw me," the girl said. "My mother's home, when she comes to the door I can surprise her." Putting her forefinger to her lips, the girl admonished Kerri not to tell. So, Kerri knocked on the door, and when the widow came, the little girl's plan was carried out flawlessly. Kerri was invited in for tea, and the little girl, who turned out to be named Lily, was told to play in her room.

"Your daughter's beautiful," Kerri said, when they were settled with pungent mugs of Golan tea.

"Thank you," the widow Sharon said. "She looks just like her father."

"I'm sorry..."

"No, don't be sorry," Sharon said. "That's part of why I came here. I couldn't stand living with people who didn't think Lily and I could manage on our own. I miss my husband... I miss him most for Lily, because I know she'll barely remember him when she's grown. But...we're fine." The widow toyed with her tea bag for a minute. "I'm telling you this," she said, "because the sooner you know it, the better we'll get along."

Kerri was surprised by Sharon's forwardness, but she appreciated it.

"Now, let's not talk about our pasts anymore," Sharon said. "Let me show you my greenhouse, my future."

Kerri rose and followed Sharon out the back door, through the edge of her backyard, and to the door of the greenhouse. Sharon stopped then and said, "You may want to leave your jacket out here. It's quite warm inside." Obligingly, Kerri hung her jacket on a convenient hook outside the greenhouse door.

Inside the greenhouse, huge lights hung from the ceiling and sat, squatly, on the floor. They flooded the entire area with orange light and a warmth so thick it made the air dance. The heat, at first, felt unbearable to Kerri, but she adjusted quickly. Seen in the right frame of mind, she realized, the heat was relaxing like a warm bath. After a few minutes in the greenhouse, Kerri even started to wonder how she'd managed to not feel cold outside.

The plants, of course, were all suited to such intense heat and light. They were also, Kerri noticed, almost entirely fruit and vegetable producing varieties. It was as if Sharon had come intending to feed the starving peoples of Heffe, deprived of good fruits and vegetables by the coldness of their dying sun.

"You like?" Sharon asked.

"I do...you have quite a setup." Kerri looked closer at the organized tangle of plants: vines stretched across the floor and grew right up the trunks of various small trees. Every plant was laden with fruit: it hung from the trees, grew from vines on the floor, and Kerri was sure she could find it growing among many roots. "But, why..." Kerri eventually brought herself to ask, "did you bring all of this here? Surely there was a better world, one more suited to the plants you grow?"

Sharon smiled a coquettish smile. "I have a plan..." she began, and probably would have continued if Kerri hadn't inadvertently interrupted to say:

"I mean, even if my husband...I mean," Kerri corrected herself, "*when* my husband saves Heffe VIII's sun, this world will never be naturally suited to these plants. They'll always need a greenhouse here."

"Your husband is the specialist here to save the sun?" Sharon asked. "I should have realized that..."

"He's been working at it for years," Kerri said. "But, he seems to be very close."

Sharon smiled sympathetically. She clearly didn't believe Kerri that Alan was getting close. Kerri fought against her impulse to defend her husband. Confused by Sharon's sympathy and wanting to remove the spotlight from herself, Kerri asked stumblingly, "Your plan...tell me what your plan is...?"

Sharon looked for a moment as if she'd speak but held back considering some unknown thought. Eventually she settled on saying, "Perhaps I'll tell you when I know you better. For now, it can be the mystery that keeps you coming back to visit."

Kerri smiled and laughed, happy to realize she'd made a new friend, enigmatic though she might be.

BAURY and his sister's pups were already waiting outside as Kerri flew her hoverpod up to their house. They were all going to Lily's seventh birthday party. Apparently, Lily went to school in Ques'trian, and she'd met Baury's two nieces and one nephew there. They weren't as old as Lily, but they were the only Heffen children she knew who spoke any English. Lily could speak the Petriezski tongue better than Alan, but she liked having friends who also spoke English: they could use it as a secret code when around the other Heffen children. Keeping secrets, and flaunting them, was fun.

"Thanks for picking us up," Baury said as the little ones filed in to the back of the hoverpod. "I never could get the hang of flying these things."

Once the nieces and nephew were strapped in safely, Kerri started the hoverpod toward Sharon's estate.

"So?" Baury asked. "This is the first time you've seen my nieces and nephew...aren't they handsome little troublemakers?"

"Flat-faced as any Golan, just like you hoped they'd be," Kerri replied, paying more attention to steering than to the little ones in the back seat.

"What's with the tree?" Baury asked, indicating the potted kitty-willow tree, packed tightly in the back, its uppermost branches straining against the hoverpod's ceiling.

"That's my present for Lily," Kerri replied. "I painted the pot myself."

"A tree?" Baury said skeptically. "Most young girls prefer toys other than trees...or so I've been told."

Kerri smiled enigmatically, a trait she'd begun to pick up from Sharon. Baury would understand when she gave the tree to Lily. Kerri knew she would love it. A tree like that belonged in the possession of a little girl who would really enjoy it. Nonetheless, Kerri had felt a pang of regret as she'd dug it up from the center of her garden. She'd never gotten around to showing Alan the kitten-seeds... It always seemed like there'd be another year. She almost wished she'd gone with her first impulse, and merely grafted a cutting from the tree onto a healthy root ball. Then, she could have kept her own kitty-willow while still giving one to Lily. It was better this way. It felt like a rite of passage.

The hoverpod pulled up in front of Sharon's estate, parked, and opened its side doors. Kerri, Baury, and the young ones got out. Kerri went to the back of the hoverpod to unload the tree, and Baury stayed to help her. The nieces and nephew, however, ran straight for the front door, eager to be playing with their human friend and joining in the birthday party games.

As Kerri carried the large, ceramic pot, hand-painted with playing kittens, Baury walked beside her. He began asking after Alan, how he was doing, whether he'd seemed different lately. Kerri answered that he Alan was, as always, busy. Perhaps, he seemed more anxious than usual, but Kerri knew of no reason to be concerned.

"There is a reason to be concerned," Baury said, ardently. "Alan probably doesn't know this yet, since Trenti just told me..." Baury waited a moment as Kerri put down the tree, and knocked on Sharon's door. "The most recent plan failed. They can't keep the strong force constant changed for long enough. It always collapses back to normal."

Kerri was genuinely concerned. It would be hard for Alan to learn this... Before Kerri could say anything, she was flustered to find Sharon at the door, bidding them to come in. Kerri pushed her worries aside, picked up the potted tree, and went looking for the birthday girl.

Baury stayed close to Kerri, so he was there when she described the kitty-willow tree and its yearly crop of kitten-seeds to Lily. He was less than impressed, but he could see the wonder in Lily's eyes.

"How soon?" Lily asked, eager to play with the promised dozens of tiny kittens.

"It'll be a few more weeks, maybe a month, before it blooms again," Kerri said. The disappointment of having to wait showed through Lily's otherwise impeccably polite thank you. Still, Kerri felt a joy in watching Lily examine her new tree that rivaled the joy she'd felt as a child at owning one. Perhaps the senses don't dull with age, she thought. They find new sources of delight.

Baury coughed, reminding Kerri of his presence. "A very nice gift," he said.

"It was my favorite...of all the gifts I got during my childhood." Kerri turned to face Baury. "What will they do?" she asked, returning to her worry for Alan. "Is there another plan?"

"There is another plan," Baury said. "It's dangerous. It's been tried on other suns..." Baury trailed off, looking pensive. "It has a tendency to change the course of dying suns: instead of dying, they inflate, rapidly, into red giants."

Kerri looked horrified, so Baury quickly added. "There would be time, a few months, maybe a year or two, to evacuate the planet. No more long and lingering death...the world growing colder while we cling to it. People would have to leave and leave quickly."

"Unless it works, right?"

"Unless it works," Baury agreed.

"Why are you telling me..." Kerri began but couldn't finish.

"I'm worried about Alan," Baury said, taking Kerri's hands in his own and pressing them, looking up at her face earnestly. "He has a very hard decision ahead of him... If you can, I want you to convince him that we wouldn't blame him for making the wrong choice. We all know our sun is dying..." Baury broke off for a minute, his small ears flattened against the top of his head. "We asked Alan to help us, but it's not his fault if he can't. Will you tell him that?"

Kerri agreed that she would.

KERRI HOVERED outside Alan's home office, her hand resting on the doorframe. She could see Alan inside, sitting at his desk, his head leaned over his work. Lately, he was always working. Kerri didn't want to disturb him. She really, really didn't. But, her promise to Baury still hung over her, and by now she was sure Alan knew of his last plan not working.

Over the last few weeks, Alan had grown increasingly irritable. His moodiness and growing depression suggested to Kerri that Baury was right: Alan was feeling the immense weight on his shoulders of having to make a decision that would affect an entire planet's population.

There were no excuses for waiting left. Kerri had to talk to him and make good on her promise to Baury. Maybe it *would* make Alan feel better.

Kerri came into the room, walked up behind Alan, and placed her hands, lightly, on his shoulders. She began rubbing the tightened muscles, but Alan shouldered her away. "I'm very busy..." he said.

"I know, but, we need to talk," Kerri said.

Alan, still facing his work instead of Kerri, closed his eyes in exasperation, and repeated, "I'm very busy."

"Alan, I know that," Kerri said, pushing against Alan's shoulder, turning him around to face her. "I know about the decision you have to make, and I want you to know it'll be all right however it turns out. The people here know that you're not a god...just a scientist, and they won't blame you if it goes wrong."

Alan looked at Kerri with hardened eyes, repressing all the frustration he'd been feeling. He didn't speak.

Kerri continued, saying, "You know I'll stand by you no matter what. In fact, if the sun does go red-giant... You know I've never learned the language here... I won't mind if we have to move away."

The hardness in Alan's eyes narrowed to a burning. "You're expecting me to fail," he said, bitterness in his voice.

Kerri was astonished. Her mouth dropped open, and then she pulled herself together enough to speak. "You know that's not true... I've always believed in you..."

"It's that witch," Alan said in almost a shout. "That widow-witch has turned you against me. She's a vulture who's just been waiting for me to fail, and she's made you just like her!" Alan turned violently back to his work, and Kerri was left, standing behind him, her arms fallen slack beside her, in a state of shock. Alan had never yelled at her before.

"Sharon?" she muttered, more to herself than Alan. "She never said anything about you... Baury told me to talk to you..."

"Then the witch has turned him against me too. I never liked your friends, Kerri," Alan said, surprisingly calm, without turning towards her.

For five, maybe ten, minutes Kerri stood in Alan's office. He didn't turn around or speak to her again.

Kerri locked the door to their low-grav bedroom before turning the gravity down that night. In the early hours of the morning, she heard Alan try the door. Lying alone in the dark, floating lightly on their bed, she heard the doorknob rattle, unwilling to turn. Kerri caught her breath. She was afraid Alan might beat on the door, order her to let him in...she'd never felt afraid of Alan before. Instead, he left without even knocking. Kerri sobbed herself to sleep.

∼

KERRI WAS WORKING in Sharon's greenhouse when the news came. Sharon knew she'd have to break it to Kerri, who had been isolating herself from everything but Sharon's greenhouse garden. She came over early every morning and left late every night. Sharon knew there was something wrong, but she was too sensitive to ask Kerri. Kerri would tell her when the time came.

The news Sharon received was this: Alan's final, brilliant attempt had failed. Alan and his colleagues had slowed the sun's rate of rotation, decreasing its centripetal forces and causing the sun to shrink in on itself. The hope had been to push the sun back on track as a young, yellow dwarf star with many millions of years ahead of it, again. Instead, the once yellow dwarf would soon expand into a red giant, but not over the usual time span. No, the inhabitants of Heffe VIII had only a few short years to evacuate, finding new homes in a universe which had dispossessed them.

As Sharon told Kerri, Kerri began to cry. Sharon was worried for her, but, then, Kerri had been crying a lot lately, so Sharon wasn't sure if she was crying over Alan's failure or not. Sharon gave her a hug.

"You expected this to happen, didn't you?" Kerri asked, trying not to feel betrayed. "That's why you brought these plants here...these plants that need a huge, hot sun..." Kerri broke down crying again, and Sharon led her out of the greenhouse, led her into the house, and sat her down with a mug of Golan tea.

"Nine times out of ten," Sharon said, "the experts who are hired to save dying suns end up expanding them, artificially, into red giants. I didn't expect Alan to fail...I just knew the odds."

Kerri stared into her steaming mug of tea. She was thinking about the flowers she had found, waiting for her, every morning since her and Alan's fight. Every night she locked the bedroom door, and every morning there were flowers waiting for her on the other side. Alan had never mentioned the fight.

"Artificially created red giants are the best kind for what I'm planning to do," Sharon continued. "I'm sorry that Alan failed...I would rather that he'd succeeded and that I'd had to find a different sun..."

Kerri traced her finger around the rim of her mug. She dipped her finger into the hot tea and it stung. "Why are artificial ones better?" Kerri asked, trying to be interested, trying to think about Sharon instead of Alan.

Sharon was watching Kerri closely and growing more worried by the minute. "It's time to tell you my secret," she said. "Remember?" she asked. "I said it was a secret, to keep you coming back here. Well, now's the time."

Kerri managed to look up, her interest piqued by the mention of a secret she'd long forgotten.

Sharon continued: "I'm going to make a garden on the sun...on the surface of the sun."

"Can you do that?" Kerri said.

"If you have the right technology: solar force shields and radiation osmitters; they're very expensive and hard to come by. They're also hard to put in place. That's why artificial giants are better...you can fit the shields on them as they grow," Sharon replied. "It's been done before...a few sun-gardens have been very successful. There's so much energy at the surface of a sun...the plants grow like crazy. You'd hardly believe it."

Kerri tried to imagine standing at the surface of a sun, orangey-red light glowing around her, blotting out the eternal night sky above. She imagined the super-hot plasma sloshing beneath the force shield under her feet and plants growing everywhere. She asked, "Can I come?"

THE SWOLLEN red sun of Heffe VIII hung in the sky over Ques'trian's space port. The asphalt landing strips boasted far more spaceships than they'd seen at one time ever before. Long lines of Petriezski men and women, along with many Heffen of other nationalities, waited to board ships that would take them away from their home. The planet was more than half deserted now.

Kerri walked with Alan towards the lines, watching the sad faces around them. She wondered where most of these dispossessed would go... She wondered how much of their culture would survive. Baury along with his sister and her family were heading for Crossroads station. That was a good place, but a space station isn't the same as a world when it comes to making a home. Still, it would be a good place to start out.

Kerri found the line she was looking for and led Alan there. The bags were already packed and loaded on board. Now, all that was left was to get in line and wait.

Kerri looked at Alan, standing beside her. His shoulders were slumped in the same dejected posture they'd held for months. He was a broken man, and Kerri felt horrible for what she was about to do. She had loved him.

Once she could see Baury and his family in the distance, coming towards them, she knew it was time. She drew a deep breath, and, standing a foot back from Alan, she started to say:

"Alan, there's something I have to explain to you..." It would be easiest to just say it fast: "I'm not going with you. I'm going with Sharon...to garden the sun..."

Alan looked at her with disgust in his eyes. She was afraid of all the things he wasn't saying, yet, glad not to hear them.

"I made sure your ticket was on the same flight as Baury's," she said. "I've asked him and Trenti to look after you." Kerri wanted to say something more. She wanted to explain all the thoughts and feelings she had...she wanted to say something that would make it all better. She'd felt that way for months. There was no magic cure.

She and Alan had been growing away from each other for a long time. She doubted now that they'd ever known each other well. Maybe if he'd apologized with words instead of flowers... Maybe if he'd just asked what was wrong... Maybe... There were too many *maybes*. Kerri felt trapped when she thought of them.

Finally, Baury and his relatives caught up to Kerri and Alan. Kerri felt relieved to see his charming, flat face. "Oh, Baury," she sighed. "I'm glad to see you." They hugged each other, exchanged a few words of chitchat, and agreed, wholeheartedly, to keep in touch. Kerri said goodbye to each of the little ones and smiled at Trenti and the sister.

As Kerri backed away, starting to leave, she said to Baury, "Do look after him," and, to Alan, she just said, "I'm sorry."

She didn't wait for a response.

Sharon and Lily were waiting for her, outside the hatch of their own ship, the only ship heading towards instead of away from the sun.

"I'm ready," Kerri said, running towards them. "That was hard..."

Sharon smiled sympathetically and put her hand on Kerri's back, guiding her into the ship. Once they were seated inside, Lily pulled on Kerri's sleeve.

"To cheer you up," Lily said, holding out a kitten-seed on her palm. Kerri took the tiny cat and cupped it in her hands. It was going on a voyage grander than any a kitten-seed had gone on before...

"You brought your tree?" Kerri asked.

"Of course," Lily said. "Can you imagine how happy the kittens will be on the sun?"

Kerri imagined the little seeds, curled up, stretched out, in all a cat's many poses, basking *on* the light of the sun. "It's a perfect place for them," Kerri said. It's a perfect place for *me*, she thought. It was horrible leaving Alan...she wished the Alan she remembered, from when she was young, could come. He wouldn't like it there: just plants and gardening.

Plants and gardening...

"It's good to be doing something you care about," Sharon said, piloting the ship into liftoff, rising through the atmosphere, breaking into the sky, and heading for the sun.

As the red giant swelled into view, Kerri knew she was going to her true and final home. She felt an excitement usually reserved for children.

2

―――――

LIFE WITH THE TUMBLERS

The boy didn't know how long six months would be. He was only five, and it sounded like forever. His mother, however, knew exactly how long six months would be. She could measure it out against the milestones of her life. It was the time between a kiss and the promise that bound her and Derrick together. It was the time between deciding pregnancy was unbearable and finally bearing Kyan. She *knew* six months. It was too long, and not nearly long enough.

"I hope you know what you're getting into."

Arlene brushed Derrick's worry aside with an amused shake of her head. "Of course, I don't. That's why I'm going. Complete immersion in the tumbler culture is the only way to really progress my studies."

"I just hope you're not too busy taking notes on those savage tumblers to look after Kyan."

Kyan looked up from the fortress he built on the floor: "Is Uncle Sleatoo a savage?"

Arlene grimaced. "They're not savages."

"Neither is he your uncle," Derrick told Kyan. "I don't want you calling him that."

"Don't worry, I'll make sure that your son remembers he's a human boy and not the nephew of a plant." Arlene moved closer to Derrick, slipping her arm around his back. "What're you really worried about?"

Derrick enfolded her in his arms. "I just want you to be careful out there. I'm not used to having you and Kyan so far out of my sight."

Arlene kissed her husband reassuringly, and whispered in his ear, "We'll be back before you know it."

The rest of the evening passed in a blur of preparations. Arlene planned to leave at dawn because it gave her sisters-in-law less of a chance to interfere. She knew they were afraid of the tumbler town, and she didn't want them filling Kyan's head with nonsense stories right as they were about to leave. Until now, they'd held their tongues, not believing she'd go through with it. Tomorrow, it would be too real, and she knew they would make a scene.

In the dark of morning Arlene finished the last minute packing, and Kyan played a game he called "packing." He put a few of his toys in and out of his own little knapsack, while Arlene packed everything he'd really need. Sleatoo met them at the edge of town, and Arlene entered a different world. That morning she'd been the wife of a farmer, and secondly she'd been a scientist. From the moment she kissed her husband goodbye, sending him out to work the fields, she was on sabbatical and could be a scientist first.

THE TUMBLER VILLAGE glowed with balls of light in the distance. Sleatoo told her the balls were hives of sun-bees, kept by a caste of beekeepers. Sleatoo's closest relative was a beekeeper, but

Arlene didn't understand the relationship between them. In six years of talking to Sleatoo, Arlene could never get far enough past the language barrier to really understand the familial structure of tumbler society.

Tomorrow she would see it, and the abstract words she knew of Sleatoo's language would finally have concrete images to hang on.

"Why didn't Sleatoo stay to dinner with us?" Kyan asked.

"The tumblers don't eat like us, honey. They absorb light and minerals into their leaves."

Kyan wrinkled his nose, not understanding.

"Sleatoo says they have bathhouses, and when they soak in the mineral treated water, all the food they need soaks into them."

"It's like if I put my hand in the soup?"

"Yes, honey, careful," Arlene brushed Kyan's hand away. "The soup's hot." She was cooking it over their portable camp stove.

Even during sabbatical from being a wife, being a mother never stops.

DURING THE DAYS, Arlene and Kyan moved among the tumblers. Arlene equipped her son daily with the raw materials to amuse and feed himself in the foreign landscape of the tumbler town: educational drives for his com-pad and a pack of bread, cheeses, and smoked meat. As the sun went down, they shared a hot meal over the camp stove, beyond the fringe of the tumbler town. But, during the day, Kyan was his own keeper.

Arlene worried. She trusted her son, but she didn't know what rules to give him, since she didn't know what transgressions would offend the tumblers.

Arlene watched the tumblers in silence, scribbling notes

into her notebook. The tumbler way of life entered her eyes and exited through her fingertips. Her notes tantalized with the promise to coalesce into a whole string of academic papers. Once she got home, she'd have the raw material to keep her busy for months going on years.

Yet, she couldn't expect Kyan to carry on, quietly, as she did: young boys need to play.

Against every grain of her anthropological training, Arlene allowed Kyan, at the beginning of the second week, to join the tumblers in their bathhouse. His happy splashing echoed merrily through the town and left mineral water sloshed on the floor. The tumblers soaked, dancing their sustenance dances, the same as they had before—albeit rocked by Kyan's waves.

"He is a new kind of weather," Sleatoo assured her in his haunting, piping imitation of a human voice. "We take the weather here as it comes."

Arlene found reassurance in Sleatoo's expression. The purple tube leaves and greeny vines that vibrated when he spoke and the flower-like blue parts, which were open wide, seeing her, nestled at the nexus of Sleatoo's long, bending limbs. No side was up, because each limb took its turn as foot and as arm when a tumbler walked. Thus, the leaf-like sensory organs grew thick at the hub of the limbs, each type many times repeated, and enough types that Arlene still didn't understand them all.

No other human alive—except for Kyan—could have found a face in the shrubby center of a tumbler, but Arlene found expressions there.

"Doesn't your village have children?" Arlene asked, wishing for a companion for Kyan. At home, he had seven cousins to play with him. Here he was all alone. "Do they play like Kyan does?"

"Children are rooted."

"You grow from the ground? Where?"

So, Sleatoo showed Arlene the nursery.

TUMBLER HOMES ARE platforms at the tops of tall poles. Rungs stick out from the poles, creating a spiral ladder. Some platforms are glassed in; others are not. As far as Arlene could tell, the difference depended on the preference of the individual tumbler. All tumblers lived alone; they never shared a platform.

But, tumblers grow up quite differently.

The nursery was one of the two largest buildings built on the ground, entirely walled with glass like a greenhouse. The other was the center of the adult community: the bathhouse, where tumblers met to soak, dance their sustenance dances under the water, converse, and carry on the business of the town. It was like the church, town hall, and saloon all rolled into one.

"I grew here," Sleatoo said, extending the slender end of his most convenient limb towards the back corner of the nursery. "It's why they call me *shlivilee*. It means 'one who grew in a corner.' They say it's why I'm shy, why I spend my time visiting your colony."

"How do you mean?"

"When you grow in the center, everyone talks to you. You are the center. Only Kliassara, my beekeeping sister, talked to me. She grew here." Sleatoo gestured to a space a little out from the corner; a location cutting the corner off from the rest of the open room.

"You got less practice socializing," Arlene said. "Everything is determined by physical location... Aren't there any children who don't grow here?"

"If we find stray seedlings, we transplant them here. Children are tended here. Talked to; taught. But, there are always wild ones. They are grim and silent, and don't know our ways.

They come out of the forest, and sometimes join a village. Sometimes they stay wanderers, but they're always welcome. They're strong from growing up alone and surviving. We village-dwellers admire that."

Arlene put down her notes. "I'm confused," she said. "Where are the children?" She looked at the stiff, leaf-bare tumblers crouched around the room. "These? Are these them?"

"No!" Sleatoo exclaimed with the shaking and tinkling of his ginger-colored leaf parts that signified laughter. "These are the old ones who are waiting. They're ready to move on, so they're waiting for the next crop of children."

"So there are no children now?"

"Oh, there are. We've had flowering dances here several times since the last crop. They're waiting underground."

"They haven't sprouted yet?"

"Right."

Arlene sighed. Kyan would have to make do without play-mates, even rooted ones, for a while longer.

COME THE THIRD MONTH, Sleatoo left his human charges alone in his tumbler town. Wanderlust struck his heart, and he set out for the human colony. He took his usual pack of tumbler goods to trade, but he also bore messages from Arlene and Kyan to their husband and father.

Without her guide, Arlene found that her tongue had less of a hold on the tumbler language than her ear. At times, she resorted to signs and gestures to make herself understood. Finally she realized that Kyan could hum, sing, and whistle the tumbler language as proficiently as if he had all those bizarre leaf organs hidden in his throat instead of a single tongue. He'd been listening to Uncle Sleatoo tell him stories since infancy, and the sounds seemed natural to him.

"Which tumblers do you like talking to best?" Arlene asked her son. If he was to translate for her, she wanted him to enjoy it.

"The old ones in the nursery," Kyan said. "They play pirates with me."

Arlene asked if she could watch them play, and Kyan told her she'd have to be the wicked sea witch guarding the gold. "The treasure's at the bottom of the sea," Kyan explained. "We're in boats all the time in the nursery."

Playing pirates turned out to mean that the stiff, old tumblers watched Kyan run around the nursery and listened to him describe his exploits. "We're cannonballing the sea witch!!!" or "I have to get the water out of my boat..." He knelt to the floor and pantomimed bucketing water.

When Kyan tired himself out, he sat in the dirt and listened to the tumbler ancients' stories. It was a culture of reminiscence: rather than living life, these tumblers had resigned themselves to retelling it, reanalyzing it, finding peace with it, and preparing to leave it. They seemed truly grateful for the fresh audience Kyan provided. Perhaps that's why they lived now in the nursery? Perhaps they were waiting for the new tumblers to sprout?

"My favorite is Sleatoo's granddaddy," Kyan confided as they walked back to camp.

"How do you know," Arlene asked, "that he's Sleatoo's granddad?"

"He talks proud of Sleatoo, and tells stories about him all the time. Like you said my granddad talks of me."

They both looked at the stars, and Arlene tousled Kyan's hair. "You'll meet him someday. Someday we'll all go on a trip. You, and Daddy, and me, and we'll go see your granddad."

Although, honestly, Arlene had to admit that arranging to visit her homeworld would be ten times more difficult than arranging this sabbatical in the wilderness. She felt a twinge, realizing that her sabbatical was now more than half over.

THE COMING caravan raised a ribbon of dust Arlene could see hours before she interpreted it. She kept looking up from her notes to squint quizzically at the skyline, but she didn't understand until Kyan emerged from his pirate lair. He summed it up in one word: "*Cousins!*"

Nothing would do but to run and meet them. Arlene put aside her work and trailed behind, wondering what could possibly have gotten into her sisters-in-law. Whatever in the world could drag them across the wilderness to a place that scared them? And whyever hadn't Derrick stopped them?

"My god, but you've come a long way," Arlene called when she got close enough. Kyan, running ahead, had already joined them. He was part of the many armed, many legged, many voiced band of children.

"Nothing better for tiring out the little ones!" came the call back from Gina. Derrick was walking beside her.

Derrick smiled when they met, took her hand, and said "Surprised?"

"Yes," Arlene answered, but her accompanying smile was half-hearted. The smile half was for seeing Derrick; the worried half was for all the children and the havoc they might wreak on the tumbler town.

The reunited spouses didn't have time to talk. Gina was doing all the talking for all of them: "I see why you went away now!" Gina's speech was punctuated by inarticulate commands and reprimands to her children. "Why, Derrick's missed you so much, Leanne and I were getting jealous. Our husbands are so used to us, they barely pay us the time of day!" Gina resettled the toddler on her hip. "Thought we'd kill two birds with one stone. Derrick gets to see you again, and we see if we can't make our husbands miss us too."

"My camp's not really set up for visitors..." Arlene began, flustered, but Gina smiled broadly and dismissed her objection.

"Don't you mind that. We'll take care of everything. You just focus on that work you're doing," Gina wrinkled her nose as she said it, "and spend time with Derrick!"

"Thanks," Arlene said and looked over at Derrick. With her face turned away from Gina and while Leanne was busy with the children, Arlene mouthed the words, *"Why did you bring them?"*

TRUE TO HER WORD, Gina and her sister Leanne took care of everything. Arlene's once unimposing camp—a butane stove and two sleeping bags under the stars—was transformed. Gina pitched tents, and Leanne built a bonfire; Kyan and his cousins created a ruckus, running like bandits, screeching like banshees.

Before beginning the bonfire, Leanne pulled Arlene aside. "*They* won't mind, will they? Gathering up wood... bracken... we won't accidentally burn any of their children." Leanne looked nervously at the tumbler town in the distance. "Will we?"

Arlene blushed at her sister-in-law's ignorance born of prejudice. "You would know if a ball of bracken were a tumbler," she said. "It would roll away." Neither Gina nor Leanne belonged out here.

Though, Arlene had to admit her own ignorance: the idea of a bonfire made her nervous because she had no idea how the tumblers would react. She never saw them make fire themselves, and she kept her own fires small. Discrete. Yet, the tumblers must have some relationship to fire. Was it taboo? Or unimportant? Ceremonial? Possibly as part of a ceremony Arlene hadn't seen? She had to have her notebook...

Arlene sat herself down away from the chaos and pored over her notes, hunting for details she might have recorded but ignored. Clues about the tumblers and fire.

In time, a shadow loomed over her, long in the setting sun, and its source scuffed his feet in the dust. The light was already dim, and Derrick's shadow made it hard to read. However, Arlene didn't want to talk to Derrick right now. If she did talk to him, she would just snap at him for turning her quiet camp into a circus. So, she strained her eyes and held her tongue.

Nonetheless, Derrick joined her, sitting on the splintery log. "You're doing a good job with Kyan here," Derrick said, but Arlene merely frowned at her notes. "He's thriving. He's learning real independence." Derrick paused, waiting for Arlene to jump in. When she didn't, he rattled nervously on. "Gina's kids and Leanne's kids—they're such apron-string holders. Don't get me wrong, I love my nephews and nieces. Every one of them. But, Kyan, he's the pick of the litter. And it's no stretch to see why," he smiled, "with the way that you look after him."

Arlene finally looked up to see Derrick expectantly watching her. "You're mad," he said. After a moment, he added, "I'm sorry."

"Yes, but what for?" Arlene asked, testing Derrick to see if he knew what he'd done.

"For making you angry."

A long drawn out sigh. "You don't know?"

"Sorry," he shrugged. "You'll have to tell me."

Arlene closed her eyes and spoke in even, measured tones. "Bringing a child on an anthropological field study is unorthodox, but, as you say, Kyan is an exceptional child. I can trust him." Arlene's eyes opened and fixed directly, angrily on Derrick. "However, Gina and Leanne's children—not to mention Gina and Leanne—are *completely* out of control." Her volume mounted with her anger, though she tried to control it for the sake of appearances, in front of her sisters-in-law.

Continuing in a forced hush, she said, "I have no idea what kind of damage they could do to the tumblers or their town. Let alone my ability to objectively research. Why did you bring them?!"

"That's what you're mad about?" Derrick sounded genuinely surprised. "They wanted to come."

"Of course, they didn't." Exasperation colored every timbre of her voice. "Gina is terrified of the tumblers, and Leanne keeps asking me when my studies will be done so we can hire a mercenary fleet to wipe them out." Arlene could see that her points were hitting home. She continued, "They both weed their gardens religiously, afraid that any stray weed might grow up to be a tumbler who'll sneak into their house and steal the babies away. Why, I repeat, did you bring them?"

Derrick couldn't seem to find an answer. "Look, my sisters may not know much about the tumblers or *anthropology*," he meted out the word, syllable by syllable, making it sound unreasonably scientific, "but they're good women. And they're your sisters now, as surely as they're mine. I don't see the problem with them wanting to visit you."

"You're deliberately misunderstanding me," Arlene said. Derrick insisted that he was not, and Arlene had little patience for listening to him. Their fight fizzled to a slow halt, and Arlene begged the need to return to her work. Derrick excused himself to spend time with Kyan, and the two spouses parted in mutual bafflement and frustration.

DIM EVENING DEEPENED INTO NIGHT, and the darkness threw Leanne's bonfire into sharp relief. Flames licked the sky, and

Arlene had no trouble throwing herself into her work. For, while the children sang and Derrick spent time with his long absent son, the tumblers slowly approached the circle of firelight.

They moved like a sleep-walking forest. Their slowness, the swaying, waving of their limbs, half-hidden in the dark, gave an impression of unreality. Did the trees really move closer? Or was it a spell woven by weary eyes and the intoxicating heat that shimmered as it rose into the sky?

Tonight, on this world, the trees did move, and their movements were a dance. They circled, staying in the dusky edge of the light. They moved in rhythm with one another. They kept time to a silent beat. Arlene raced to sketch all that she saw— every position, every pattern in the dance.

She hardly noticed when Gina and Leanne shepherded the children to bed. Kyan joined his cousins in a tent, gleeful, giddy with the other children's companionship.

Derrick was the last to bed, and as he went he said, "This tent is ours. I'll be waiting."

But Arlene slept under the stars.

THE SUN and Arlene rose early. She stowed her sleeping bag as it had been the night before, so the others would be none the wiser. Leanne was the next one up. She started the fire and made a minimal breakfast, before Gina joined them, bringing some of the younger nieces and nephews with her.

A rustling in the older children's tent announced Kyan, Jared, Dean, and Lana's imminent arrival. As soon as they finished eating, they explained that Kyan meant to show them his "pirate's lair" today.

Gina was nervous about them going into the tumbler town alone, but Leanne gave them her permission. Arlene consented as well, after making Kyan promise they'd go straight to the nursery, where the elders could look after them. Gina folded, and the children went merrily, skipping on their way.

"What if the tumblers hurt them somehow?" she asked after they were gone. "What if they get all tangled up in one of them?"

Arlene assured Gina that couldn't happen, but Gina continued with a whole string of imagined worries. Each more ridiculous than the last.

"Look," Arlene said, "the tumbler town isn't any more dangerous than our own." Gina looked skeptical, and Arlene realized she was missing the perfect opportunity to escape a morning of gossip and babies in the camp while waiting for Derrick to rise. "Tell you what," she said. "I'll go after the kids and make sure the tumblers don't hurt them." Gina looked happier already.

ON HER WAY to the nursery, Arlene stopped by the bathhouse looking for Sleatoo. She wanted to ask him about the tumblers' strange dusk dance from the night before.

Standing on the threshold of the great mineral bath, Arlene leaned toward the water and called out Sleatoo's name.

Slenderly extended branch-arms waved above and below the water's surface. Was the sustenance dance different today? Arlene thought the patterns were changed. Then they clearly did change: a single figure made his way to the edge of the pool. His branchy arms lifted him out of the water.

Fine, dewy drops ornamented Sleatoo's limbs and leaves. They bedewed him like a morning flower and fell from him like his own rain shower.

"You've flowered," Arlene said, forgetting everything else in her wonder.

More than the dew of mineral water, Sleatoo was now decorated with grand, white, dahlia-like flowers. His inner, sensory leaf-parts flattened at her comment: if he were human, he'd be blushing.

"I'm sorry," she said. "I don't mean to embarrass you. I just didn't know you ever flowered. It's beautiful." Arlene looked about her and realized most of the tumblers bore flowers now. Sleatoo had never visited her in this state.

"I stay here when... when this," he said, his sensory leaves flattening even further.

Arlene was lost to his embarrassed fumbling. She was staring at the dance and the others. She wished she had her notebook or recorder, but her memory would have to serve. She looked about eagerly, trying to take it all in: the choreography of the dance, and, *oh!* the sun-bees in the air. How had she missed their persistent hum? They flitted over the water, alighting and ascending from emergent branchy arms. They formed their own ballet, amidst the larger tumbler dance.

Sleatoo broke Arlene from her reverie. "Why did you come?" he asked, still looking uncomfortable. "I expected you to be busy with your visitors for many days."

Sleatoo's question came as a cold shock. "Is that why you agreed to bring them?" she asked. "To keep me away from the... flower time?" She'd never felt unwelcome in Sleatoo's life before.

"No, no, you misunderstand," Sleatoo said. "No one else minds you seeing the flower time. The others... They revel in it. But, well, I'm embarrassed even among my own." The slim tips of Sleatoo's limbs twisted in nervous curlicues. "Anyway," he added, "this flower time was unexpected. It's not the usual season. So, I couldn't have brought them as a diversion. Even if I'd wanted to."

Something in Sleatoo's tone made Arlene wonder if he had been planning a diversion for the "usual season." Her feeling of rejection by Sleatoo combined with her unresolved anger at Derrick, and Arlene snapped: "Then why did you bring them!?"

Unused to yelling, Sleatoo instinctively drew back. He reshaped his limbs like a tree contorted by growing away from a constant, harsh wind. "I brought them because they asked. Was I wrong?"

Abashed, Arlene said, "No, you weren't wrong." It wasn't Sleatoo's fault that Derrick had been so foolish. And she couldn't blame him for wanting his privacy. "But, don't they bother you? Your town is so peaceful... And they're so fast and loud."

Sleatoo shrugged his many, branchy arms. It was an impressive gesture. Although it was entirely human in origin, Arlene felt that a 'shrug' looked better on Sleatoo than it ever looked on a human. "Noise doesn't hurt us. Sun-bees are fast and loud too. We're not bothered by them."

Yes, Arlene thought, *but sun-bees are small.*

As Arlene approached the glass-walled nursery, her mind stayed with Sleatoo and the other flowered tumblers, dancing in the water. Her visitors were already affecting them. An *unseasonal* flower time? That could only have been caused by last night's bonfire. How much more could her visitors affect the tumblers before she was no longer studying the tumblers, but merely their effects on them?

Arlene was interrupted by Kyan emerging from the nursery, running at a breakneck pace. Lana followed him, lagging behind, clearly unable to keep up.

"Mom!" he cried, seeing Arlene.

Lana gave up the chase, yelling the word 'tattletale!' in place of bodily pursuit.

"Slow down, there, buddy," Arlene called out. Then, as he arrived, panting at her feet, "What's wrong?"

"You've got to stop them," Kyan said. "I was coming back to tell you."

"Tell me what?"

Then Arlene saw the flames rising in the distance, the nursery filling with fire. At the sight, Lana put her hand to her mouth and gasped. Kyan merely whimpered. "They had matches. They were *playing* with them."

"Oh my god…" Arlene spoke to the flames, deaf to Kyan's confession. She ran towards the building, her heart in her throat. "Dean! *Jared!*" But the horror didn't end when her nephews emerged. She could see the tumbler elders flailing in the fire, their branchy limbs trailing it.

"*What have we done?*" Arlene said, feeling all the fault herself. She fell to her knees, weeping. Like guilty puppies, the children gathered around her.

It was horrible that the fire was beautiful.

It was worse when the other tumblers began to arrive. They came from the village, vibrant in their flowers, to watch the nursery blaze. This was the end of her relationship with them. What a petty consequence to be concerned with… The wise, reverend elders had been so kind to Kyan. Such unequal repayment she'd given them.

"Look," Lana pulled at Arlene's sleeve. "They're dancing."

"Which?" Dean asked. "The burning ones or the watching ones?"

"All of them," Lana returned.

Jared shoved his sister. "Don't be stupid."

"Wait, Mom," Kyan said. "Lana's right. *Listen* to them." Kyan began chanting in the tumbler language, keeping rhythm with the song and dance. "I don't know this song."

"You understand them?" Dean asked with disdain in his voice but awe in his expression.

"Change... or seasons... they're singing about... I don't know, but they're all singing it. I can't quite make it out. Mom, do you understand?"

So, Arlene listened, and she looked at the fire with new eyes. "It's a rite of passage," she said. "The elders' last dance... is a fire dance. They were waiting... No, they couldn't have been..."

What would have happened if her nephews weren't dangerously careless with matches? The elders wouldn't wait forever. Arlene's eyes sought and found a detail in the architecture she hadn't noticed before. A long, thin metal antenna stretched from the roof of the nursery up to the sky. *A lightning rod.* She muttered to herself, though Kyan overheard, "They were waiting for a fire."

"So... we did a good thing?" Kyan asked, a tremor in his voice. He was clearly thinking of Sleatoo's grandfather and how he'd miss him.

"*No*," Arlene said emphatically. "You should never play with fire." She could see Kyan was on the edge of tears. She took him in her arms and whispered in his ear, "Sleatoo's grandfather was ready to die. He was waiting for it, but I know he liked telling his stories to you. You made the waiting easier."

Kyan nodded and held back the tears but not the quiver in his lip. Arlene squeezed him in her arms, kneeling among the abashed but entranced children. As she knelt, watching the fire dance, she heard Derrick's voice yelling from behind.

He ran to his wife and son, and put his hands on them appraisingly. Seeing that they were alright, he stood in front of Arlene and the children, placing himself between them and the perceived danger. He looked about frantically, eyeing every nearby tumbler, tensed to fight. Or flee.

"Derrick, it's okay." Arlene stood up beside him, pushing his fisted arms down, and winding her fingers between his to unclench the fists. Seeing the fear in his eyes, she finally understood why he hadn't come alone. She touched his face and said, "Oh, Derrick. I didn't know you were afraid of the tumblers."

His eyes widened and his cheeks flushed. "All I know is that my wife and son are in this town, and suddenly I see a fire! What am I supposed to think?"

Arlene gave Derrick a quizzical look. "You thought the tumblers were burning down their own town?"

"Maybe."

In all honesty, Arlene had to admit that such an assumption wouldn't have been far off the mark. "But... in an attempt to somehow threaten us?"

"Well..."

"Why would they do that?"

"I don't know!" And there was the crux of the issue.

"Then let me tell you!" Arlene yelled. "But don't come here surrounded by a swarm of children and sisters who I have to watch every moment, who I can't trust with anything!"

Derrick opened his mouth to yell back at her, but Arlene cut him off. "Don't you try defending them! That fire," she swung her arm straight out to point at the more than obvious blaze. "Your nephews started that fire playing with matches."

"Oh my god..." Derrick said. He looked at the raging fire, and then he looked at Jared and Dean. "Don't think I'm not telling your mothers." To Arlene, he said: "I'm sorry. I really didn't think... I thought you were making a big deal out of nothing. I'm sorry."

"It's all right," Arlene said, her head falling tiredly in her hands. "We were lucky." She explained about the elders and their final song.

"I really do need to take them all home," Derrick said. Arlene just barely refrained from saying, "That's what I've been telling you."

The reconciled couple gathered the four children around them, and Arlene led them all through the deserted tumbler town, back to the camp. She desperately wanted to stay with the tumblers and watch their fire dance, but her own life took precedence.

BACK AT THE CAMP, the adults all agreed: based on the turn of events, it would be best if the visitors left as soon as possible. Arlene suspected that Gina and Leanne were secretly relieved. Kyan, however, was shocked and heartbroken to discover his cousins would be gone by the end of the day. It was a hard blow, following so fast after the loss of the tumbler elders. At least, he was allowed a few more hours to play with his cousins.

While Gina and Leanne rolled up tents and re-packed other supplies, the children drew designs on boulders around the camp with chalky embers from the burned down bonfire. Meanwhile, Derrick and Arlene sat apart from the others, talking.

With her notebook open on her lap, Arlene walked Derrick through her notes. By teaching him as much as she could about the tumblers, she hoped to chip away at his newly uncovered xenophobia. If he knew the tumblers as she did, he wouldn't be afraid of them.

LONG BEFORE NIGHTFALL, the whirlwind of relatives was back on its way. That night, for the first time, the tiny camp—a butane stove and two sleeping bags under the stars—felt sad and lonely instead of adventurous. Kyan colored it that way.

"Will Daddy bring any of my cousins with him when he comes back?" He'd lain in his sleeping bag silently for forty minutes, but Arlene knew he hadn't fallen asleep.

"No, honey," Arlene said. "I'm afraid not."

"Not even Lana? Or one of the babies?"

Kyan cried a little before he slept, but he still fell asleep hours before his mother. Arlene kept thinking her way back through the day, cringing at how close they'd come to disaster, and thanking her lucky stars for how it had turned out. She hoped Gina and Leanne weren't too mad at her for not wanting them. They ought to understand after their eldest sons' antics. Either way, Derrick would tell her about it on his next visit. A visit he would make alone.

SMOKE still clung to the air. The charred ground was damp and steaming. Nursemaids had brought buckets of water to damp it down. "The seedlings will be thirsty," Sleatoo said. "Their thirst brings them up. It becomes unbearable after the fire, and the only way out seems to be up."

"How long does it take?" Kyan asked, eagerness in his voice. He'd quickly gotten over his horror that the elders' ashes were the very fertilizer for this new generation.

"Don't get too excited," Arlene admonished. "They might be too young for you to play with. We don't know how fast they grow." Turning to Sleatoo, she asked, "how soon do they learn to talk?"

Sleatoo's leaves quivered with excitement. "Look!" He contorted his many limbs to point, like magnetic field lines, at a single spot on the floor. "This leaf is the first tip of a new *shlivilee!* A child who will grow where *I* grew. Kyan, will you pay particular attention to him?"

Kyan nodded resolutely.

"Do you mean they'll be... out... and talking, before we leave?"

"Of course. Once the fire comes, it is only a few days before the seedlings come up." Sleatoo stretched himself out taller, to bring his center closer to Arlene. He focused his visual leaf parts on her. "The seedlings have been listening to the elders talk for months now. They won't know how to talk themselves at first... but, it comes quickly. Maybe you'll stay longer, to study them?"

"Maybe," Arlene said. Now that Derrick planned on visiting at least once a month, staying longer suited her fine. There was more than enough work to be done. However, she was still worried about Kyan.

"What do you think, kiddo?" Arlene asked. "Do you want to stay out here longer than our three months? Or do we need to get you home to your cousins?"

Kyan was too busy to answer. He was on his hands and knees, examining the tiny shoots of green springing up from the floor. It eased Arlene's heart knowing that he would soon have playmates again. "I guess," she told Sleatoo, "we'll have to wait and see."

3

SUMMERS ON SYLVERRA

The ship shifting into orbit woke Tara up, but she kept her eyes closed, listening to her parents talk.

"It always scares me coming here," Tara's mother said. "Your dad makes such beautiful illusions for Tara. I'm afraid some day that she'll choose not to come home."

Tara was curled up on the ratty old couch on the back of their starhopper's bridge. It was a loveseat and not meant to be slept on; she barely fit on it anymore. Her parents were sitting in the pilot and co-pilot seats, right in front of the viewscreen that must have shown the emerald and azure sphere of Grandpa Brent's planet, Sylverra.

"She's always come home with us before," Tara's father said.

In the silence that followed, Tara was perfectly certain that both her parents were thinking about the year that Tara was ten. Even though that was already five years ago. So unfair. She didn't think they'd ever stop holding it against her.

That summer, Tara had made friends with one of the little girls in Grandpa Brent's gengineered elven villages. The elf girl had hair so pale, it was nearly silver, and everything about her face was narrow and pointed: eyebrows, ears, and chin. She and

Tara had played all summer, thick as thieves and the best of friends.

When Tara'd had it explained to her that, since the gengineered elves aged much faster than normal humans, her friend would be a grown woman by the time they returned next year, she threw the most horrible tantrum. She nearly insisted that she would stay and live with Grandpa Brent, at least through the rest of her elven friend's childhood. In the end, it was her friend who convinced her to go—already, she'd been more mature than Tara and rapidly losing interest in their childish friendship.

Since then, Tara had been much more circumspect about befriending the gengineered elves. They were fun-loving, easy-going people—they'd been designed that way by Grandpa Brent, kind of like a humanoid version of dogs—but Tara had reservations about getting too close to anyone with a lifespan shorter than a healthy housecat's.

"Look," Tara's father said, "there's only a year until Tara applies to Wespirtech. She's so excited about going there with her friend Jenn that I don't think she'd give that up." Brandon lowered his voice, conspiratorially, and said, "Though I'll be shocked if Jenn gets in. But Tara doesn't need to know that."

Tara opened her mouth to object and defend her friend, but then she remembered she was pretending to still be asleep. If she defended Jenn, her parents would know she was listening.

"Besides," her father continued, "if Tara did decide to stay, well, she couldn't get a better education in gengineering—even at Wespirtech. And I trust my dad to take good care of her. We've talked about this. He raised me. And for all his eccentricities, he was a good parent."

"I know," her mother said. "It wouldn't be so bad. She'll be going away to college soon anyway. In just two years. I guess, I'm just so used to being afraid of Brent's illusions. It would have broken my heart if she'd really insisted on staying here when she was younger—choosing to spend her childhood with her grandpa, forcing me to either let her go, move here too—" Tara's mother shuddered at the mere thought. She enjoyed visiting, but she wouldn't want to live on Brent's world. "—or be the evil mother who puts her foot down and breaks her daughter's heart."

Suddenly, Tara felt bad listening in. Every summer, throughout her childhood, she'd known—sort of—that Grandpa Brent and Mom were fighting over her. She loved the creatures that Grandpa Brent gengineered for her, but when Mom said it was time to go home, it was time to go home. Sure, she'd drag her feet and try to bargain for a few extra days of summer with Grandpa Brent—what kid wouldn't?—but she hadn't meant to make her mom worry that she'd rather be raised by her grandpa.

The silence stretched on, and Tara fell asleep again. When she awoke, the starhopper was already parked on the planet, next to the summer house that Grandpa Brent had built for her family before Tara was even born.

"Come on, honey," Tara's mother said to her. "You'll sleep better if you come inside."

But Tara was done sleeping. It was a strange twilight hour on this part of the world—Tara wasn't sure if it was dusk or just before dawn, since she hadn't paid attention to where the sun was as they landed. Either way, after days cooped up on the two-room starhopper, Tara was ready to get out and explore. After helping her parents bring in their bags from the starhopper and fending off repeated parental offerings of food —breakfast, since apparently it was dawn—Tara took off towards the closest elven village.

Tara strolled easily through the grassy meadows, where the waist-high blades of grass parted for her, bowing away from the tread of her feet and changing color slightly, turning a richer shade of emerald as she passed. Tara had always wondered whether Grandpa Brent had bred the grasses to do that so her father, Brandon, was easier to keep track of back when he was a little kid. It's hard to run away when the grass itself keeps a record in darker green of where you've walked. Of course, the darker paths faded after an hour or so. Still, that was plenty of time to catch a wayward child. There had been times, when Tara was younger, when she'd spelled out words in the meadows with her paths or made squiggly patterns or simply run back and forth, back and forth, trying to darken all the grass. It had been like a giant etch-a-sketch she played with her feet and could only see properly if she climbed up one of the trees and looked down.

Fortunately, Grandpa Brent had bred some excellent climbing trees with knobbly branches that were easy to grab onto and get good footholds on; on the climbing trees, the branches started nearly at the ground and spiraled around their trunks like spiral staircases.

Sylverra was a magical place, designed especially to delight Tara. Well, actually, Grandpa Brent had designed it to delight himself, but Tara was a child—a teenager now—and it still seemed to her that a world which had existed long before she was born—or her parents had even met—must have been designed specifically for her, especially because it had been made by her grandfather. Adults' lives revolve around children, even before those children exist, don't they?

The elven village looked much the same as it had every summer before, at first glance. The cute thatched-roof huts and the communal cooking fires were all the same. It was a deceptively low-tech village, considering that everything on this corner of the planet had been designer-made. But then, it's easy to live a low-tech, low-impact life when everything around you has been designed specifically to accommodate you. The plants that grew wild these days had once been specifically cultivated, bred to grow here and to grow edible fruits, roots, stems, and leaves. A complete, healthy, and delicious diet could be grazed from nuts and berries that simply waited for human-like hands to pluck them.

As the elves themselves began waking for the day and coming out of their huts to join Tara beside one of the fires, she started to see some of the differences from the previous summer. The youngest elves—babies and toddlers who'd been born since last summer—had darker skin and hair than Tara had seen among the elves before. Looking more closely, she saw that the darkness was a greenish cast, and when she asked, one of the older elves informed her that—on their request—Brent had helped the elves add photosynthetic genes to their DNA. This new generation could simply lay in the sunlight and absorb energy as it streamed down from the sky. Half plant, half person.

"I could alter your DNA the same way," Grandpa Brent's voice said from behind Tara. "If you'd like."

Tara's face broke into a beaming smile. "Grandpa!" she cried, standing and whirling about to face him and then fall into his arms for a big bear hug.

"Come," Grandpa Brent said, after the hug was over. "I'll show you what else I've changed during the last year."

Tara followed her grandfather around like a duckling following its mother as he showed her ladybugs that glittered like rubies living among the emerald grasses—but not metaphorically, they really looked like little living rubies—cats with feathered wings folded against their sides, and a dragonfly large enough for her to ride. Though Grandpa Brent wouldn't let her ride it. "I've hard-wired docility into the giant dragon-flies' behavior, so they wouldn't purposely hurt you... but they don't really understand having riders yet. So, you'd need to be geared up properly for a lot of falls before it'd be safe to ride one."

"I'm willing to wear safety gear," Tara answered eagerly.

Grandpa Brent just shrugged and said, "Maybe later. I did a flight test with one recently, and I'd like to spend a few weeks working the kinks out before doing another."

Tara accepted her grandfather's determination without objection. That had always been how things worked on Sylverra. Grandpa Brent was god here, and if you wanted to enjoy his garden of wonders, you did what he said. That's how Tara's father, Brandon, had been raised. Her mother, Caitlyn, had more trouble accepting it. She'd grown up on a normal planet with actual cities full of people, not some weird backwater world where literally every sentient creature had been created by one mad scientist, drunk with his own abilities, high on his own power. That's how Caitlyn described her father-in-law. She wasn't wrong.

None of the creatures on Sylverra had asked for Brent Schweitzer to blend up their DNA like a fancy cocktail and call them into existence. But then, children never ask to be born, not exactly, even when they're unexpected. Parents simply decide to have them. And Brent had decided to make a magical world, filled with creatures and plants that reflected his own artistic, aesthetic mind. He did his best to brew their personalities from strands of DNA that led to creatures grateful for their lives, rather than ones furious with the lots they'd drawn. Even the elves—fully humanoid, sentient beings—had been designed carefully to be naturally happy, cheerful people who didn't struggle with the shortness of their own lives. Kind of like many dogs, who can be terribly smart while still basically loving life and not being overly worried by life's problems—a reflection of how their brains are built. Though, even so, Caitlyn had concerns about the ethics of her father-in-law's world and generally stayed mostly away from the elves, finding their sunny dispositions unnatural and creepy. Not everyone likes dogs. And Caitlyn was more of a cat person, inherently wary and a natural skeptic. The elves' contentment made no sense to her.

Tara understood contentment when she was on Sylverra. She felt like she understood why her grandfather had run away from the Human Expansion and secretly created his menagerie on this world. He'd had a vision. A beautiful vision. And during the summers, when she was here, she could lose herself inside it.

Days passed into weeks, and the summer wore on. Tara spent less time aimlessly exploring the fields and forests than she had when she was younger, less time among the elves—who were busy with their own lives—and instead spent more time following around after her grandfather.

Tara was intrigued by what she'd overheard her father say: that she could get as good of an education from Grandpa Brent as she could at Wespirtech, the premier institute of science and technological innovation in the entire galaxy. If that were really true... it was worth thinking seriously about. So, instead of simply playing and enjoying her vacation in paradise, Tara pressed her grandfather to explain everything he could to her. She learned about genetics; she learned about the tools he used to edit genes, and the way altered viral bodies could be used to propagate edited genes throughout an already developed body.

But also, in between the times Tara spent trailing after Grandpa Brent, she hung close to her mother, trying to absorb every bit of information she could about her mother's discomfort with Sylverra. It was tricky, because Caitlyn clearly had no intention of speaking poorly about Tara's grandfather in front of her. She'd spent years holding her tongue. She was good at it. She wasn't going to slip up easily now. And Tara couldn't easily repeat the circumstances of their arrival at Sylverra for this summer, when her mother had thought she was sleeping.

So, eventually, as summer turned from a bud to a fully

bloomed flower, Tara realized she'd have to confront her mother directly.

"Why don't you like Sylverra?" Tara asked her mother, without any preamble, in the direct way of a person young enough to have not had her edges blunted and worn away by society yet.

Tara's mother looked surprised. She'd been working on a complicated puzzle that involved a lot of different colors blending into each other on subtle gradients; as she made progress on it, the whole thing was turning into a beautiful sculpture. Tara's family had several sculptures—originally puzzles—that had been designed by the same artist that they'd done during previous summers and had become decorations in their summer house here once finished. This one was by far the most difficult and ambitious. And for a moment, it looked like Caitlyn was going to avoid her daughter's question by simply pretending to be too absorbed in the puzzle to think about it. But then she said, "I don't dislike Sylverra."

Tara cocked an eyebrow in a particularly teenaged expression of skepticism. Caitlyn glanced up from the puzzle long enough to see it, sighed, and said, "Okay, I don't love it, but so what? Why do you want to know about how I feel about Sylverra?"

Tara had an in. Once she got her mom talking, she knew how to keep her mom talking. So, she sat down on the far side of the puzzle, fiddled with a few of the more strangely shaped pieces that hadn't been attached yet to any of the gracefully curving abstract shape that was coming together, and muttered something indiscernible about elves and feelings and getting older and loving her grandpa, ending with, "And I'm a lot like Grandpa, so I guess I'm just worried that if you don't like what he's chosen to do with his life, you're not gonna like me."

Caitlyn sighed really deeply in the way that only the parent of a teenager can. She tried to center herself and steady herself and not fall for her daughter's bait. "Your grandfather has created something really beautiful here," Caitlyn said, trying to keep herself on steady ground. If she started by stating a fact, her daughter couldn't argue with her. Not easily. And she wanted to keep this from turning into an argument. Conversations turned into arguments with her daughter so easily these days. "But..." Caitlyn knew the ground she was walking on, conversationally, was about to get shakier. But she was going to do her best to direct Tara's argumentative side away from her. "...have you ever wondered by your grandfather makes all his fantastical genetic... uh... inventions here? Instead of, you know, back among the planets of the Human Expansion? Back among civilization?"

Caitlyn could see her daughter's brow squinch at the question, trying to figure out if she should bristle or lash out. Instead, Tara simply frowned, pondering the question. Then she asked, in an even, non-argumentative tone, "Is that a problem?"

Caitlyn shrugged. She had asked herself that exact question many times. If there was nothing wrong with what Brent was doing, why was it out here? Why was it a secret? Why was he a fugitive who she was never supposed to mention? Sure, when she'd started taking her relationship with Brandon seriously, and he'd mentioned that he was—super-secretly—the cloned son of the famous Brent Schweitzer who'd stolen a ton of equipment from Wespirtech and then disappeared for thirty years before the authorities had found him dead (supposedly) on a faraway planet, she'd read everything she could about Brent, including several biographies.

All of those books had asked the question: why? Why did he take off with all that technology? And of course, once Caitlyn had really become a part of the family, marrying Brandon, she'd found out half of the why. The answer was Sylverra.

Brent Schweitzer had stolen a top-of-the-line spaceship

loaded with as much high tech equipment as he could cram into it so that he could fly here. To Sylverra. Clone himself and raise the baby under the name Brandon. Gengineer the elves, the color-changing trees, the butterflies with poems inscribed on their wings, unicorns, gryphons, and every other fantastical biological life form he could think of.

Caitlyn knew the practical answer to why Brent Schweitzer had stolen a spaceship. She knew what he had done with his ill-gotten technologies. She knew the answer to a mystery that people had tried to solve for decades.

But she still didn't know why he couldn't have just stayed at Wespirtech.

As a child, Caitlyn had had a pet cat with fur that changed color with its mood. She'd named it Rainbow. And even back then, as a small child, she'd known that her pretty pet was thanks to some nearly-mythological, larger-than-life, disappeared scientist named Brent Schweitzer. Yes, he was still that famous. And yes, the work he'd done at Wespirtech still filled the worlds of the civilization he'd left behind. Nearly every arboretum had a whole section devoted to the flowers he'd gengineered. Most schools employed one of the Keats, a specialized type of extra-intelligent parrot, as a language tutor.

Wespirtech had taught Brent, sponsored him, and subsidized his work. And then, instead of staying there, where he could have done work that would do people some good, he'd simply disappeared. Instead of curing diseases, he created designer butterflies that no one but himself and his elves would see. Instead of creating gene therapies that would change the lives of people throughout the western spiral arm of the galaxy, he helped the elves he'd gengineered with their whim to become photosynthetic.

He could do so much good.

And instead, he played games and pleased himself.

Caitlyn didn't want to say any of that to her teenaged

daughter. But she kind of wished Tara would be able to see it for herself.

Finally, Caitlyn settled for saying, "Your grandfather is a brilliant man, but sometimes, when we're here... I look around, and all I can see is him. He's made himself a world, and everything in it reflects him. He's set himself up a private planet where he can play god. And I don't believe in gods."

Tara narrowed her eyes in thought, and Caitlyn felt the sharpness of her expression like a dagger of judgment. She was being judged by her daughter for her own judgment of her father-in-law. She hoped, in Tara's eyes, she measured up. She hoped her discomfort with Brent wouldn't turn into a wedge between them.

Tara carried her mother's words like a pendant hung around her neck, always with her, always reminding her of her mother's opinion, as she walked through Brent's world for the next few days. She looked at the color-changing grasses and the trees whose leaves vibrated and sang like the sound of a stringed orchestra tuning. She spent time in the elven village, even talking with the woman who used to be her childhood friend. Summers ago. A whole season of an elf's life ago. She had her own daughter now, a green-haired girl who ran wild, causing delight everywhere she stumbled.

Tara didn't see her Grandpa Brent reflected in any of the world around her. Sure, he had grown the original elves in clone vats—lifetimes ago, more than her own life ago, back when her father, Brandon, had been but a boy—but the elven village had taken on its own life since then. Tara saw how Grandpa Brent was treated by the elves—a funny, quirky elder who had specific knowledge he could use to help them with arcane projects. They didn't treat him like a god.

He might design the butterflies who had poems inscribed in their colorful wings, but once they hatched from their eggs, he set them free. They flew among the trees, untouched by anyone they didn't choose to let touch them. They became a part of the world. Not part of him. He'd made a place, and he lived in it, maybe occasionally adding to it... but he wasn't a god, and he didn't pretend to be.

Even so, even if Tara disagreed with half of what her mother had said, she decided to carry her mother's question to Grandpa Brent. On an afternoon when he was noodling around with the genetic sequences for a butterfly-winged pegasus in his laboratory—a weird, small building that seemed to be one giant piece of lab equipment with shining screens and tempting buttons covering its inside from end to end—Tara asked with the same abruptness she'd used to such great effect on her mother, "Why don't you come back to civilization?"

"What?" Brent asked, seemingly only half-listening to his granddaughter and still mostly focused on the strings of letters streaming across the glowing screen in front of him.

"Why do you have this weird, isolated little lab out here?" Tara elaborated. "Why don't you go back to Wespirtech?"

"Hmm?" Brent still wasn't looking at Tara, but he added, almost like it was an afterthought to speak aloud when answering someone else's question, "I'm a fugitive, remember? That's why you can't tell anyone I'm out here."

Tara frowned. She'd heard this story before, but it didn't really hold up. She'd taken too many civics classes—and listened to her parents rant about what was being left out of those civics classes—to fall for the idea that Brent Schweitzer wouldn't be able to buy himself back into the good graces of society if he'd felt like doing it. There were far too many valuable innovations on his world, in this laboratory, and inside his head for him to truly be unable to rejoin the broader society if he'd wanted to.

So he must not want to.

And Tara could understand that. He'd made himself a wonderland here. But it didn't entirely feel real.

Sylverra was the place she went for summer vacations. The people who lived here were living life on a different scale, and because of that, the pacing and fabric of their lives was different from hers. The children got to be adults faster, and the adults enjoyed the time they had, but few of them seemed interested in building their society any further than the complacent utopia that already existed.

Tara wasn't sure yet how she fit into society at large. Like the pieces in the puzzle her mother had brought with them, she was a piece that didn't have a clear place yet. But she thought, probably, she did want to be a part of the broader puzzle, not left off to the side, creating an entirely new world of her own. Or trying to fit into her grandfather's.

And yet, as her father had said, so many weeks ago, when they'd just been arriving, there was a lot she could learn from someone like her Grandpa Brent. If she could convince him to teach her.

"Hey, Grandpa," Tara said, "can you show me what you're doing?"

He was still fiddling with a computer screen filled with readouts of a strand of DNA. "What? This?" he asked. "I'm making sure the back muscles on these unicorns will be strong enough to control the butterfly wings I'm designing for them."

"Will they be able to fly?" Tara asked.

"No," Brent answered easily. "The wings will look beautiful and will help them cool themselves, but they'll never be strong enough for actual flight."

Aesthetic. Impractical. Just like everything else about Sylverra. Everything else Grandpa Brent made. Tara could see why her mother found him frustrating. But he was still her grandfather. And even if she only visited Sylverra, Tara was glad it was here, being beautiful and arcane, defying the strictures of the rest of the universe.

"Don't you want to run off and play?" Grandpa Brent asked,

finally seeming distracted by his granddaughter's presence. "I think some of the unicorns have foals you could find."

"I'd rather learn about how you designed them," Tara said, pulling a stool up beside her grandfather. "If you're willing to teach me."

Grandpa Brent shrugged. "Whatever floats your boat," he said, before launching into a lecture so dense with biology and gengineering terminology and concepts that it made Tara's head spin. He clearly wasn't going to take it easy on her, just because she was a kid. And, whatever her mother thought, he didn't seem interested in winning her over. He made the delights that lived in his garden of wonders for himself—for the universe, simply so they would exist—not because he was trying to steal his granddaughter away to keep her here. He was too lost in his own world to play games like that. Besides, if he'd wanted another child to raise, he could have cloned himself again.

Brent had never been a threat to Caitlyn. Tara didn't think her mother would believe that, but it wouldn't matter what she believed. When the summer ended, Tara would go home with her parents, but maybe, she'd take along a little extra knowledge with her.

4

THE PARABLE OF TWO QUEENS

The guards backed away, cautious, ready to intervene. The diplomat raised his eyebrows, hopeful. Unfortunately, the aliens didn't stay still for long. The Zi'rai representative launched herself at the Zee'nee, and their fight broke out again. N-jointed arms flailed and mandibles snapped. The four human guards flew into the fray and laboriously re-separated the aliens.

The Zi'rai, with her dramatically striped carapace, strained against the guards. Her brilliant stripes catching the light, the Zi'rai cut an imposing, bellicose figure. It took three guards to hold her. The Zee'nee, however, cowered. His deep purple carapace blended into the shadow cast by the one guard, Crewman Davis, standing over him.

"Take them away," the diplomat said, lowering his head into his hands. "Three of you guards take the Zi'rai to cellblock gamma and keep a two man watch over her at all times. Crewman Braieden, take the Zee'nee to cellblock alpha. I'll join you shortly." The diplomat stumbled over the word "crewman"...it always felt weird to call his one woman guard by that title.

"Commander Dyall, Sir," Braieden objected, "I already have a good hold on the Zi'rai, sir. Why not send Crewman Davis?"

"Whatever's easiest." Then, turning to his Keat translators perched on their stands, the diplomat Dyall added: "Babbette, you follow the Zi'rai; Jude, you go with the Zee'nee. See if you can make more progress on their languages. Everyone dismissed."

"Yassir," chimed the Keats.

The guards began with their myrmecoid charges down the hall. Jude, with his gray feathers, and Babbette, with her designer colored feathers—a more recently gengineered Keat—took to the air and flapped after them.

The diplomat, alone now, slid forward, slumping against the negotiation table. He thumped his forehead lightly against the cool surface. Negotiations were not going well. Negotiations were not, he corrected himself, going at all. He'd dealt with intractable delegates, but he'd never before dealt with delegates so deeply committed to their war that they continued it in one on one combat.

For the moment, the situation was under control. The delegates were separated. Warships flanked either side of Dyall's diplomatic dinghy. The warlike Zi'rai ship was pinned against an asteroid. The Zee'nee ship wasn't giving any trouble. Still, it was an unhappy status quo.

Maybe Dyall couldn't get the delegates talking to each other, but he could at least talk to the two of them. Getting a few of his multitudinous questions cleared up would be a real start.

～

STANDING before the Zee'nee's cell, Dyall looked upon the many joints, the dull sheen, the smoothness and intricacy of the Zee'nee's body. It was like a finely tuned, well-oiled machine.

Dyall tried not to think of it as a war machine... but after watching the delegates fight, it was hard to think of it any other way.

Looking at such efficiency, Dyall felt clumsy and lumpy in his own body. Even Crewman Davis, standing beside the cell's door, looked odd, his shape unsuitable to its task, in contrast to the Zee'nee. Some alien races are so efficient, Dyall thought. He wondered if human bodies seemed that way to any of the aliens he'd met. It would have surprised him, partly because he felt so tired.

"Ask the Zee'nee whom it represents," Dyall commanded Jude.

In response, the gray-feathered Keat screeched an incomprehensible jumble of sounds. Those sounds made more sense in Dyall's ears when he saw the Zee'nee respond in kind. The exoskeletoned creature looked up, mouth parts moving. His mandibles and smaller mouth parts clacked and clattered in a sound like fireworks exploding: a large boom, a crackle of smaller bursts, a large boom again, and then all the sounds at once.

"Noisy," Dyall muttered to himself. "What did he say?"

"I represent my Queen, Her Highness who would be deeply offended to know that You Who Promised Diplomacy have instead worked in league with the Zi'rai Queen's Lowness. Should that You know that Her Highness will not make sacrifices to reclaim my humble self. There are many drones on Her ship, and She will not suffer greatly at my loss."

The Zee'nee drone watched Jude repeat his speech. As Jude finished, the Zee'nee folded his highly segmented legs around himself. The armored head, with drooping antenna, was held low. Vestigial wings on the back of the Zee'nee's carapace spasmed fitfully.

"How am I in league with the Zi'rai queen?" Dyall asked, fearful of finding the Zee'nee unwilling to speak. Fortunately for Dyall, the Zee'nee continued to be bound by duty to the queen he no longer expected to see again.

"When that You requested diplomats, my self of a drone was sent. Drones are to deal the Queen's dealing with drones, but You That Sent has subjected me to the attacks of a warrior."

Dyall shook his head, trying to understand the Zee'nee through the hobbled sentences Jude kept translating. "If my guards manhandled you, it was only to protect you from the Zi'rai delegate..." But that wasn't it. The Zee'nee was upset about the Zi'rai. Warriors? Drones? Myrmecoid races tend to be caste based societies. "Did the Zi'rai queen send a member of the wrong caste to be a diplomat?"

The Zee'nee did not respond.

"You and your queen have my sincere apologies for offending you. I am not knowingly in league with the Zi'rai. Whether you believe it or not, I represent a disinterested party."

For a few antenna twitches the Zee'nee drone's head remained low. Then he spoke: "Perhaps you do not, truly, understand... I will trust. May my Queen, Her Highness, forgive me if I am wrong. If You That Claim Disinterest are not in league with the Zi'rai Queen's Lowness, then She has dealt You a great insult. When the diplomacy of a drone is asked for, to send the fury of a warrior is utmost treachery. She has refused Your offer."

Again, Dyall felt the meaning in the words filtering into his head slowly. "If the Zi'rai queen sent a drone, you would deal with her?"

"With him. Yes."

"I'll get this cleared up."

JUDE ACCOMPANIED Commander Dyall to see the Zi'rai warrior. As they entered cell block gamma, Dyall and Jude passed the changing of the guard. Crewman Anders relieved Crewman Braieden, who went on her way. Babbette, the colorful Keat was inside, and greeted them.

Now knowing the caste difference between his visitors, Dyall could easily discern the bodily differences. It wasn't only the Zi'rai's attitude that bespoke aggression: her entire body was built larger, sharper, more dangerously. Also, she hadn't the vestigial wings of the Zee'nee drone. Nonetheless... The two creatures were sufficiently similar that Dyall suspected a shared ancestry. Perhaps their races had diverged, but they almost certainly grew together on one world.

"Jude, Babbete... how similar are their languages?"

The Keats conferred briefly and Jude answered: "The languages are similar enough to be two dialects of the same tongue."

Dyall nodded. He'd thought as much. Swap the one's dull sheen of purple and the other's vivid striping for plain old red and black; shrink the aliens down; and what Dyall was dealing with was two warring ant hives in the Amazon Basin. Well, not quite.

The frightening individual in front of Dyall bore as much resemblance to a terran ant as a government soldier, machine gun at his side and shades hiding his eyes, bears to a marmoset. Dyall couldn't help feeling he'd rather face the marmoset.

The discussion between Dyall and the Zi'rai proceeded badly. All of Dyall's attempts at diplomatic communion were met with the reply: "I will kill for my Queen!" If Crewmen Anders and Dawson hadn't restrained her, Dyall was confident the Zi'rai warrior would have proved her words. Probably on his body.

The Zee'nee drone was right. This warrior had not been sent on a diplomatic mission. If Dyall meant to make progress with the Zi'rai, he would have to contact their queen again.

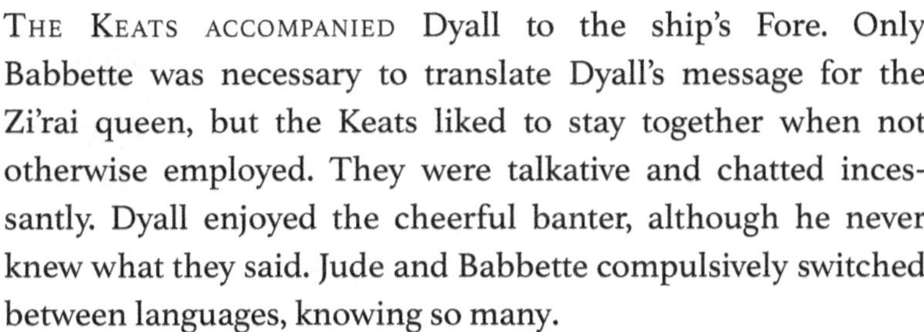

THE KEATS ACCOMPANIED Dyall to the ship's Fore. Only Babbette was necessary to translate Dyall's message for the Zi'rai queen, but the Keats liked to stay together when not otherwise employed. They were talkative and chatted incessantly. Dyall enjoyed the cheerful banter, although he never knew what they said. Jude and Babbette compulsively switched between languages, knowing so many.

"How's the diplomacy going?" Pro-Pilot Lonnie asked, swiveling her chair as Dyall entered the Fore. Crewman Braieden who'd been talking with Lonnie straightened into a salute to her captain.

"At ease," Dyall said, more to Braieden than Lonnie. The rank of Pro-Pilot placed Lonnie at a level comparable to, albeit different from, Dyall's.

"Pro-Pilot, Commander," Braieden said with a nod to each as she excused herself from the Fore.

"So?" Lonnie prompted, returning to her earlier question.

"Well, Carol," Dyall said, sinking into his own swivel chair. "Apparently the queen of the Zi'rai doesn't take us seriously."

"That's not good."

"No, it's not. Would you open a channel to the Zi'rai ship? I need to send a message to her..."

Lonnie turned to the communications controls, and Dyall wrested Babbette's attention away from her conversation with Jude. While the humans were speaking, the Keats had perched themselves on the arm and back of an unoccupied chair. Babbette memorized Dyall's message to the Zi'rai quickly, delivered it in the clamorous Zi'rai tongue as soon as the channel opened, and returned to her and Jude's repartee.

Thus, the Zi'rai queen was warned: the warrior delegate was to be returned on the shuttle that brought her; if she was not replaced with a drone delegate, dire but unspecified consequences would follow.

Fortunately for Dyall, although he would have been able, he was not forced to concoct dire consequences. The Zi'rai queen proved cooperative and the new, drone delegate arrived within the hour.

FOUR GUARDS STOOD behind two seated myrmecoids. Human chairs didn't suit the insect-like aliens, so they crouched on the floor, segmented limbs folded angularly about them. Although not especially beetle-like, the aliens took on the aspect of ancient Egyptian scarabs brought horrifyingly to life.

Now, progress would be made. "Zi'rai delegate," Dyall said, "as I have already told the Zee'nee delegate, I represent the Human Expansionist Movement. My government has important outposts and colonies in several neighboring star-systems, thus we hold vigil over the *un*claimed systems in this sector of the galaxy as well." Dyall paused, giving Jude and Babbette a chance to catch up. "The appearance of both your ships in this system baffles us. Where did you come from? Who do you represent? What is your business here?"

The Zi'rai spoke first: "The Majesty of Her Queen of the Zi'rai seeks vengeance for the loss of Her Kindred Queens. You must release the Zee'nee ship to Her."

"My Queen, Her Highness, could hold claim for similar recompense!" the Zee'nee screeched in response.

"There are more queens?" Dyall asked.

The insects seethed at each other. The Zee'nee was first to respond: "There are no more Queens. Only Her Highness has survived."

"Tell me what happened."

The Zi'rai remained silent, but again the Zee'nee

complied. "There were quakes. There were calamities. Great collapses of *space*. Time... Distance... The stars themselves... Everything shook as if to fold in on itself. My Queen, Her Highness, was clever, determined, and saved Us, Her Grateful Children. Her Highness found a rip... She took the ship through."

The Zee'nee's antenna drooped and his body lowered. Dyall waited, but nothing more was forthcoming. He turned back to the Zi'rai drone, but Dyall had few hopes of learning much from him. He had to try... "Your ship followed the Zee'nee ship through a rip in space?"

"Such cowards as They planted the seeds of the end of time! They creep away to hide while all others die? No! The Majesty of the Queen of the Zi'rai, one and only remaining monarch, demands vengeance."

Dyall drew a deep breath. "Okay. What about you?" He turned to the Zee'nee drone. "What does the Zee'nee queen want?"

The Zee'nee did not look up. "My Queen, Her Highness, wishes only quietude in which to rebuild. She is alone now. Let Her Highness weep in peace."

The dealings proceeded, but no more progress was made. The Zee'nee alone would have been easy to handle: Dyall could hand them the deed to a few asteroids in the Banti'phi asteroid field *now*. The Zee'nee could rebuild there. But Dyall couldn't allow the Zi'rai to keep fighting them, and the Zi'rai would settle for nothing less. Dyall dismissed the unmoving delegates, under guard, to their cells.

～

BACK AT THE FORE, Dyall settled down to talk with Pro-Pilot Lonnie. She listened sympathetically while he described the situation, but Dyall couldn't help feeling he'd rather talk to another diplomat. All Carol could do was listen; she couldn't advise, share similar experiences, or give true commiseration.

"I'd like to tow their ships to opposite sides of the galaxy and leave them there," Dyall said. "But I suspect the Zi'rai would wage war with everything in their path until they found the Zee'nee again..."

"At least they're talking to each other," Carol said.

"Barely. It's more like..."

"I mean that you were stuck before, and you made it better. You'll do it again."

"It's like they're talking to me... not to each other... explaining *why* they can't talk to each other." Dyall shook his head and leaned back. He emanated frustration. "Thanks for the confidence, though." The doors slid open, revealing Crewman Braieden behind them. Dyall greeted her, saying: "Crewman Braieden... what brings you to the Fore?"

"Excuse me Commander," she replied, "I didn't mean to interrupt an officer's conference. I came to speak with the Pro-Pilot, but it can wait." With a curt bow of the head, Braieden backed out of the Fore.

"What's that about?" Dyall asked.

"Nothing," Carol said. "We're friends."

"Oh. I've only seen her with the other guards."

"We keep our friendship quiet. It's hard for her, being the only woman guard."

"I try to accommodate her... Braieden takes the hardest jobs whenever she can."

"Actually," Carol paused, as if deciding whether to proceed. "You shouldn't... *accommodate* her. She's as capable as the other guards."

"I know that. I just..."

"Just don't."

Dyall wanted to defend himself but didn't trust himself to speak. He thought about Braieden with the other guards. They joked and laughed together. Drinking buddies. Dyall's own friendship with Carol Lonnie showed him that Braieden's friendship with her must be very different from her friendships with the other guards. "It must be nice for her to have another woman to talk to," Dyall said. "And for you."

Lonnie nodded but said, "she can't talk to me about current Expansionist policy like you can. But then, I never understand her descriptions of Aikido holds... We all need friends at our own level."

"That's true," Dyall said. "I don't mind admitting that I'd give a lot to have another diplomat to talk to about now."

Carol smiled sympathetically and offered to put a message through to Crossroads Station. He knew several diplomats there, but he shuddered at the idea of stilted, time-lagged conversation. There was nothing like a true face to face, in the same room, old-fashioned conversation, but it might be better than nothing. Dyall nearly accepted, when he suddenly realized he didn't need to. He'd figured out what he had to do.

Guards accompanied the Zi'rai drone home to his ship. They came with him into the presence of his queen, and Babbette delivered her message: the Expansionists had chosen to deal solely with the Zi'rai. The Zee'nee queen was to be executed, as a sign of good faith. Would the Zi'rai queen please accompany Babbette and the guards back to watch the ceremony? The queen showed reluctance, but the guards insisted. Since her ship was pinned against an asteroid by Dyall's warships, the Zi'rai queen was left with little choice.

Jude told the same story to the Zee'nee queen.

Now two expectant, myrmecoid monarchs looked at each other across Dyall's negotiations table. Finally, they were in the same room. "All right," Dyall said, secure in his knowledge of the ten armed guards surrounding them. (He'd borrowed six from his warships for the occasion.)

Dyall drew a deep breath; Jude and Babbette straightened up to begin translating. Now he would see if a shared station truly meant shared interests. "You've both been lied to. There will be no execution."

The Zi'rai queen reared her sharpest pincers. Guards raised their guns, but Dyall gestured for them to hold fire. He hurried on: "Neither of you will be returned to your ship, until you've worked out a settlement."

"There will be no... *settlement*," the Zi'rai queen spat. "Such a false and sororicidal monarch as she must die."

The Zee'nee queen hissed back an insult, but Jude could not translate it.

"Fine," Dyall said, "your ships will be turned over to their crews, and each of you will be locked up on charges of homicidal insanity."

"We have only defended ourselves!" said the Zee'nee queen.

"The Expansionists will not take sides."

"Without Us, Our Venerable Children will wither and die... there is no life for the Honest Hive without a Highest Queen..."

Dyall shook his head. Listening to such twisted and bizarrely lofty translations made him ache for normal conversation.

"Has not your Vileness an Heiress?" the Zi'rai said, taunting.

"No time..."

The Zi'rai clacked her armored legs upon the floor shifting her weight. "Nor for Us," she admitted. "Does not matter. There are no strongholds here to conquer...nothing for a New Queen to inherit."

"Our Worthy Workers build... With more time, We might make Queendoms for many a New Queen."

A pregnant pause began. Dyall looked at the queens and

could read none of their history in their alien faces. But the queens could see it. In each other, they saw their shared past.

ON A WORLD, in another universe, an insect-like species grew, changing, expanding, dividing into many races. The home-world of these races rioted with war. As they could, queens escaped into space and found breathing room of their own.

Among their native star's asteroid field, the Zi'rai, Zee'nee, and their cousins found a relative peace. One queen per ship. One queen per asteroid. Queens dealing with each other only when need be. Absolute rulers of tiny provinces.

Then the end began. The star system shook with a universe's dying spasms, and queens raced to get away. Perhaps another star would not be dying? But death was everywhere. Only one Zee'nee ship found a way out: a rip in space. An enraged Zi'rai ship followed.

Two queens, on their separate ships, stewarded the last vestiges of their race. Each found solace in her children... The workers made them proud; their warriors made them secure; and, their drones were a comfort. But none of those understood the pressures of being queen.

Now, these lonely queens were here, on Dyall's ship. If ever there was a time when two queens *needed* to deal with each other, it was now.

"We withdraw Our Royal Command. We will *forgive* the Zee'nee..."

The Zee'nee queen hissed that there was nothing to forgive, but the Zi'rai queen continued unconcerned.

"...if the Worthy Workers of the Zee'nee will...work with Our Own Worthy Workers to build."

"You mean teach them? As they are trained in nothing but

the maintenance of a festering warship?" the Zee'nee jeered, but quickly added: "Our Queendom accepts the offer."

Dyall sensed the end of his role approaching. For him, it was all paperwork from here: leasing a portion of the Banti'phi asteroid field; signing non-aggression pacts; informing the two queens of relevant Expansionist laws... For the queens, however, negotiations had just begun.

When Dyall left them, they were talking so fast that Jude and Babbette could no longer keep up. Theirs was a new empire in the making. Dyall would have to return and see it some day. Preferably as a tourist.

5

APPLES IN ARUBA

"I'll have the tuna fish." Lawrence closed his menu.

"Are you kidding?" Jeggy said. "Don't order that. It's like eating apples in Aruba."

"What are you supposed to eat in Aruba?" Lawrence eyed the other patrons of *The All Alien Cafe* suspiciously.

"I dunno. Something exotic." As Jeggy was saying it, too late for him to stop, both their eyes fell on the gentleman being seated at the table next to them. He had six crab-like legs, a carapace covered in hexagonal spikes, and a spiny, bushy, green tail. "*Something tropical.*"

Their new neighbor clacked a friendly claw and picked up his menu. He looked a little like a pineapple.

Lawrence stuck with the tuna fish.

6

EMMANUEL AND THE CANNIBALS

The second ship crash landed too.

Emmanuel knew the *Clemency* was a junker, and he was well experienced at safely crashing her. Better still, he carried plenty of spare parts, and he knew how to use them. Emmanuel was one of the best crash-pilots and jerry-rigging mechanics this end of the spiral arm. Seriously, you could not do better. Unless you didn't crash. But, that would involve owning a ship that didn't constantly blow her fuses, fuse her wiring, and otherwise complain about having to haul her titanium alloy hull through space.

As it was, Emmanuel aimed for a nice, flat, green continent on the day side of the nearest planet. No point taking chances on how long the night would last. (Little did he know it was the same continent the first ship had picked more than a century ago.) The *Clemency* landed with little added damage to her innards, cargo, or pilot. But, her hull, as always, got rather scraped up. Emmanuel had given up on keeping her shiny a long time ago. These days she was lucky if he repainted her name.

Emmanuel swung himself out of the wreck of his ship. He

figured he could fix her in an hour if he hurried. From the way she'd been acting, she'd probably blown a fuse. It was always a blown fuse, which was why Emmanuel picked them up by the mechanic's dozen (twelve good ones mixed in with two duds), every time he got the chance. Modern ships didn't have fuses, so not every starship emporium carried them anymore.

Emmanuel whistled as he worked at opening the *Clemency's* hull to fill the inhuman silence surrounding him. It was a pretty valley that hosted him, in the full growth of summer. Wind rustled in the green, but that was the only native sound he could hear.

The hull plate covering access to the *Clemency's* engine whumped as it hit the ground. Emmanuel slipped the last screw in his pocket. He liked that whumping noise, he realized. So, he followed it up with a racket. Perhaps he clashed his wrench and clattered the sprockets more than need be, but the *Clemency* was a robust ship. Her innards could take it. Still, he couldn't keep it up. Once he'd removed all the obstacles and found the core problem, a bunch of fried wires, he settled down to the fine work of splicing in replacements. Not a noisy job.

Silence is spooky, and it became even spookier when Emmanuel heard voices. They were utterly out of place in a valley lacking even the hum of insects. The chatter of birds. The croak of frogs? Emmanuel couldn't hear a single other living sound, but he heard voices coming from the trees at the edge of the valley. And they spoke Solanese.

"Hi!" he shouted. "My ship crashed! I won't be long, then I'll be on my way. I hope I'm not troubling you?"

Emmanuel didn't know about the first ship. However, he was beginning to *suspect*. At least, he suspected he wasn't alone, and he was right. The nature and origin of his fellow inhabitants still eluded him. Although, their chosen language was a strong indication that this young planet was not so innocent and virginal as she seemed to be.

"Hello!?" he called again.

Emmanuel's growing speculations were confirmed when a thin but healthy-looking, olive skinned man, dressed in scant garments made of woven reeds stepped out from the cover of the nearby trees.

"Will you come to a feast?" the man asked. "Instead of leaving, will you stay for a feast? We haven't seen...a man from the...is it still the Expansion? It was the Expansion...the Human Expansion in the stories our parents told us. Are you from...there?"

Emmanuel stared, dumbfounded. How long had these people been stranded here? The man's accent was strange but not strange enough for the strangeness of the situation.

"We are having a huge feast tonight, anyway. Please come?"

"Um..." Emmanuel straightened out his tools: the screw-driver, the wire-stripper, the soldering iron, the spool of wire. All old school. He had time to spare here, didn't he? The shipment of replacement android arms for the model 20 with the bug in their right elbows wasn't due until the end the week. "Sure." he said. "Let me finish up here. I've got to put this panel back on..."

The olive-skinned man conferred with his companions, who were still obscured from sight. He told them to go on but stayed behind, himself, to guide Emmanuel to their village.

THE VILLAGE WAS in the lee of a broken hillside, a twenty minute walk into the forest. The people, their dress, and their dwellings said "savage," but their words belied it. They had minimal accents, full vocabularies, and solid grammar. They spoke perfect Solanese.

"How long have you been here?" Emmanuel asked Denwell, the man who'd become his guide.

"On this earth?" Denwell asked. He squinted as if peering into the past: "My grandmother told stories to me when I was young... She remembered a pilgrimage, before the tribes formed, to the ship we first came in. She was very young. I think maybe her grandparents—so my great, great grandparents—may have remembered people who'd actually been on the ship and knew how it worked."

"What is that..." Emmanuel tried following Denwell's family tree backward. "Six generations?"

Denwell smiled. "My grandmother used to keep track of the past. She said when the first children were born on our world that their parents, who'd come on the ship, taught them about the broken tools and... consoles, and... computers."

"They hoped to fix the ship."

"It was a fruitless hope."

"I don't know," Emmanuel said. "From my experience, any ship can be fixed. You just need the parts and know-how. The question is: which were you missing?"

"Probably both!" a girl added, joining their conversation.

"Well, I'm good with ships, and I keep a bunch of spare parts on the *Clemency*. Want me to take a look at this crash dummy of yours?"

"Would you teach me?" Denwell asked eagerly.

"It wouldn't carry us all anymore, and who says anyone wants to leave?" the girl asked.

Denwell shot her a dirty glance.

"It's not even ours... You'd have to fight the Kambee tribe to get to it."

"True," Denwell said, followed by a tight-lipped frown. "That is a problem. Though, the fighting would bear its own rewards..."

Several young men and a matronly woman came to usher their foreign guest and his companions to dinner.

The tables were long, halved logs, flat side up. Emmanuel

was seated at the foot of one of them. What looked like three village elders, including the matronly woman, were seated at the other three ends. Denwell sat beside Emmanuel, but the girl who'd joined their conversation disappeared into the long row of villagers with their backs toward him at the other table. Emmanuel tried to catch a glance of her, but his attention was immediately dominated by questions for him at his own table.

Yes, the Human Expansion was still expanding. Yes, we'd discovered alien inhabited planets. No, we hadn't found any aliens with technology on par with our own. Yes, some of them had turned out to be hostile, but mostly when we tried to bend their cultures to fit our own. Then, there were requests...

Could he bring them art? Fine cloth? More machines? He wondered how they'd pay him, but he didn't ask. Perhaps their world was mineral rich. Perhaps not. Either way, it would be a humanitarian effort not a profitable one. As he thought about it, Emmanuel couldn't help but picture the girl at the other table in a silk dress rather than the tribal gear she sported now.

The courses came one after another: a hot broth, sautéed mushrooms, an elegant salad, baked tubers...all vegetables. The silence from before, in the valley, made sudden sense. There were no animals on this world. No insects. No fruiting plants. These people had crash-landed on a planet in a pre-historic stage of development.

Amid beaming smiles and great applause, the main course came. Two platters were carried by six men each. They were held high in triumph, above the bearers heads. Two young hunters rose to bow. For one, it was his first kill. Suddenly, Emmanuel realized he had to look away. Before the platters were lowered, he stumbled away from the tables, past the platter-bearers, and out of the main hall.

Denwell came to him, shortly, and asked, "Are you sick?"

"No," Emmanuel answered, "but I might be. I couldn't see... Was it... Were they..." He couldn't ask the question. He pictured the girl he favored, back at the table. Her black hair hung past her waist; it had probably never been cut. In his mind, her delicate hands raised the food to her lips.

"What kind of animals do you have?" Emmanuel asked. "I smelled meat. What kind of animal was it?"

Distressingly, confusion painted itself across Denwell's face. "A chicken?" He answered. "A weasel? A rat?"

"What do you mean?"

"Those are all names we call the Toovall tribe. They are animals. Is that what you mean?"

Emmanuel had his answer. In this world, an *animal* was only a word, an archaic grammatical construction. At the risk of causing great offense, he didn't return to dinner. He went straight to his ship.

THE SHIPMENT of replacement android arms arrived five days early. The proprietor of the mining colony was grateful to have his model 20s working again but not as grateful as the androids themselves. Since Emmanuel was ahead of schedule, he hung around a few days playing cards with the androids, trying to drive his recent sojourn from his mind. However, the androids' faces never revealed a stitch about their poker hands and none of them wanted a human partner for bridge. So, once he'd lost enough to make him wonder what androids spend their money on, Emmanuel went on his way.

Still, he couldn't get the girl with the waist-length hair out of his head. In his imagination, she tended a stove, raking the burning embers for a more even heat. It was dark inside the stove, lit only by a dull orange glow. His mind's eye flinched away, but he knew what cooked in there without looking.

It is easy to accept monstrous acts performed by monstrous beings. But this was like an orange-winged butterfly carnivorously sinking it proboscis into human skin and feasting on blood instead of the honied nectar that is its rightful, innocuous dessert.

Emmanuel was deeply disturbed. Either his attraction to her or her cannibalism must be fixed. He knew he should go through the proper channels and report the young world to the Expansionist Moral Authorities (EMA). He should have reported them before delivering the android arms, but he'd been putting it off. He felt involved. Turning the cannibals over to the EMA would be like taking the *Clemency* back to the dealership for a tune-up. Not that anyone at the dealership would know how to tune-up a ship as old as the *Clemency*... That was beside the point: Emmanuel was a fixit man, and he felt called to face the challenge of reforming the cannibals himself.

So, he settled on a plan. His experience keeping the *Clemency* in working order had taught him to become an expert at acquiring archaic, antiquated items. Just as new starships didn't need fuses, new space colonies didn't keep entire herds of meat animals. An organ and flesh cloning plant is simply more efficient. However, Emmanuel followed up a few connections: his fuse guy supplied a classic starship dealership; the classic ships guy supplied a historical reenactment planetary settlement; and, the history buffs kept real herds of bovinids and sheepalos.

Every kid saw vids of bovinids and sheepalos growing up. Emmanuel even had a mini-electric sheepalo that slept on the foot of his bed at night. But, he'd never seen one in person. And, in person, sheepalos are big, and bovinids are smelly. Emmanuel bargained for as many of them as he could safely and humanely carry in the *Clemency*. (He dreaded the clean-up job after the trip.) He also got thorough instructions on how to take care of them.

Back to the cannibal world!

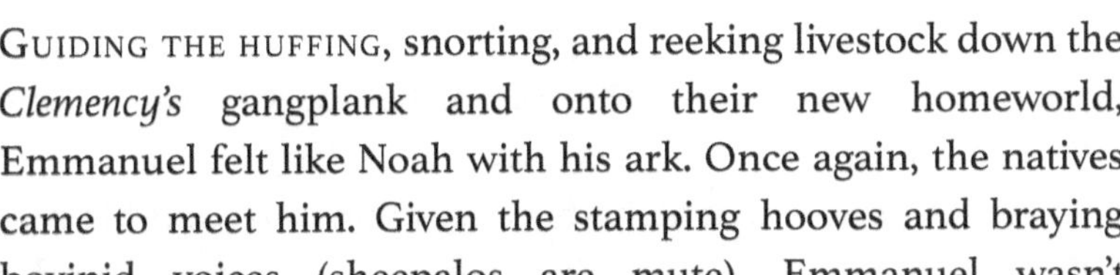

GUIDING THE HUFFING, snorting, and reeking livestock down the *Clemency's* gangplank and onto their new homeworld, Emmanuel felt like Noah with his ark. Once again, the natives came to meet him. Given the stamping hooves and braying bovinid voices (sheepalos are mute), Emmanuel wasn't surprised. His arrival had to be one of the noisiest rackets the young planet had ever heard.

"I've brought you animals!" Emmanuel declared.

People crowded around him in astonishment. Children darted forward, reaching their arms to touch the beasts, only to startle at the stamp of a hoof and run away. Denwell emerged from the crowd and came to stand beside Emmanuel. "I don't understand," he said. "These are animals?"

"Yes," Emmanuel replied. "Before you came here and forgot them, every animal name you know corresponded to a real, live beast. These are bovinids," he gestured. "And, these," he gestured again, "are sheepalos."

"We call each other 'bovinid' when we're stubborn. Or 'sheepalo' when dumb."

"Bovinids *are* stubborn. And sheepalos are dumb. That's why you use their names that way." Emmanuel saw the woman who owned his imagination among the crowd. She reached a hand up to a snuffy bovinid nose. The creature lowed and snorted hot breath into the chill morning air. Her hand settled softly under its chin. Emmanuel looked away, but he knew that new images of her would fill his mind.

"Can you read this?" Emmanuel asked, showing a comppad to Denwell. "Can you work it?"

Denwell took the comppad and scanned the files on it over the screen. It was a simple model, and the files held information on caring for the animals. Denwell looked up and nodded.

"They'll eat almost anything. That's what they're bred for."

Emmanuel didn't mention that they were also good for milking, shearing, skinning, and, especially, for eating. Denwell could read it all in the files. "I have to go now," Emmanuel said. "I want to take small herds to the other tribes too. Can you tell me where they are?"

Denwell was reluctant; he felt that Emmanuel and his gifts belonged to his tribe alone. But a visitor so powerful under circumstances so strange cannot be denied, and Denwell gave Emmanuel rough directions to the other tribes.

It was a long day for Emmanuel, tramping through forests and over hillsides, herding his gift beasts from the stars. Still, he made it back to the *Clemency* by dark, and he fell asleep satisfied in his empty ship. Meanwhile, the primitive peoples of each tribe marveled at their new bounty, and four elders, the eldest of each tribe, huddled in their lonely huts over the comppads Emmanuel had given them.

THE *CLEMENCY* DIDN'T MAKE her third landing on the little planet until more than a year later. After "fixing" the haunting images in his mind of the seductive cannibal, Emmanuel found the long-haired beauty to be merely another woman. Entirely forgettable. His great triumph, saving an entire people from their primitive, immoral ways, fell to the wayside as he found himself swept up in the day to day work of cargo-shipping. Still, his philanthropy gave him a sense of patronage, and he made time to return, bearing more gifts.

Emmanuel parked the *Clemency* in the same valley where he'd first crashed. His entrance was quieter this time, and no one came to meet him. So, he slung a pack of goods on his back and made the trek to the first village alone.

He heard bovinids, and he grinned. He felt like a hero. He walked further, and he saw bulky, furry bodies in a pen. He stopped at the pen, resting his hands on the split wood railing. The beasts looked happy and healthy, a sparkle in the bovinids' eyes and a sheen on the sheepalos' pelts.

"You've cared for your animals well," Emmanuel said to the men who were slowly gathering at the other side of the pen, quietly watching him. He noticed they still wore reed-woven clothing instead of leather. Well, they were used to it, and he couldn't expect all their ways to change overnight. Or even in a year.

"We care for them the best we can," one of the men said.

"Yes, we are very grateful," another man added.

A third man entered the pen, which Emmanuel realized wasn't fully enclosed, and placed his hand affectionately on a bovinid rump. The beast lowed and stomped, shifting its weight between cloven feet. "We love them."

Emmanuel accompanied the men into the thick of the town, noticing that sheepalos and bovinids moved freely among the huts and log-houses. Well, if they didn't run away, there was no need to fully pen them. Still, it made Emmanuel wonder what the partial pen was for.

"If we'd known you were coming, we would have prepared a feast!" Denwell came forward and gripped Emmanuel by the arm. The grip collapsed into an embrace. "It is good to see you, friend from the stars." The men stood back and looked at each other. "Although," Denwell added with some thought, "you didn't seem to like our feast so much last time."

"I think I will like it better now," Emmanuel said with a grin. "I will stay and wait for you to prepare."

"Good!" Denwell beamed. "We can show you more about our ways while you wait."

The town shuffled around him, reorganizing itself to the current plan, and Emmanuel found himself in the hands of his beautiful long-haired girl. She showed him the hut with the women weaving reeds into baskets, bags, blankets, and clothes.

Anything reeds could be used for. She took him to the kitchens, where men and women both prepared a variety of plants and tubers for consumption.

He took particular note of a bean-like plant being prepared into a curd. He had wondered how these people got enough protein given their... *unusual* diet. Clearly, they couldn't have depended on their old habits to supply enough protein, or they would have killed each other off faster than they could have reproduced. Emmanuel tasted the plant curd. It was rich and thick. It would take protein analysis to be sure, but he strongly suspected it was the answer to this conundrum.

Next Emmanuel was shown their well and, then, the lumberyard where men were splitting logs for firewood, furniture, and building materials. As they walked together, Alifia, for that was the girl's name, showed shyness in all her ways. She spoke quietly and turned her eyes demurely away when he looked at her. Emmanuel found her, once again, captivating.

They returned to the center of the village and sat beside each other, in front of the longhouse where feasts were held. A baby sheepalo who had been following Alifia like a dog came up and settled at their feet.

"This is Tiny," Alifia said. "He was the runt of the litter." She stroked the beast, and Emmanuel put his hand out to stroke it too. It reminded him of his mini-electric sheepalo as a child. It wasn't much larger. Their hands touched on the creature's downy back. Alifia smiled and, charmingly, didn't look away. Emmanuel's chest swelled with contentment.

Before the moment could be established to mean anything, a scream arose in the air around them. Another shriek, a war cry, followed from deeper in the woods.

"Quick!" a man yelled. "Herd the animals to the pen!"

Men converged on the spot, bearing weapons and herding beasts. The women and children began streaming into the log building behind them.

Emmanuel felt he should help the men, but he had no weapons and wouldn't know how to use them if he had. So, when Alifia swept Tiny in her arms and grabbed Emmanuel by the hand, he followed her docilely into the crowded building.

The women and children shuffled in the limited space, jostling each other for room, listening to the shouts and cries outside. Emmanuel was terrified, but the women and children weren't particularly fazed. Nervous more than frightened.

The fight didn't last long. A harsh rap on the longhouse door was followed by a voice crying, "They're gone."

The carnage wasn't bad—Emmanuel could catch news vids of rail gun "crowd control" on backwater planets any day, and he'd witnessed street fights with laser edged knives personally.

In comparison, stone tipped javelins and poison darts were barely dangerous. He wouldn't have been scared, Emmanuel told himself, if he hadn't been surprised. And yet, these Halloween weapons could kill when aimed right, when wielded skillfully. The evidence was before his eyes: one man and one bovinid lay dead on the ground. A wail went up among the people. Women turned their faces away and cried.

Denwell, panting from the fight, stepped forward and said, "We must prepare a proper burial. But, at least," his lip curled in an expression Emmanuel couldn't identify, "we know what we'll eat tonight." Then he directed two groups to clear the bodies away: one to the cemetery, one to the stoves.

"Wait," Emmanuel said, confused by the evidence of his eyes. "The wrong groups... The wrong groups are taking them." But no one listened.

~

Much of the village trailed after the men bearing the bovinid. They mourned the beast, reverently laying hands upon its massy side. Two men ran ahead and, with crude shovels, began digging into the ground.

"This is the graveyard..." Emmanuel said, looking around. Stones and flowers marked the burial mounds. He slowly began to understand. "What tribe was that man?" he asked.

"Kambe, scoundrels," came the bitter answer from a woman beside him.

"He was trying to steal your bovinids."

"Yes, they're very good to eat."

"Then, why are you burying this one?"

"This is Dolah," the woman said with warmth. "We loved her."

"But it's a bovinid."

"She's our bovinid."

"What about your other bovinids?"

"We love them too. You were very good to bring them to us."

"Don't you eat them?" Emmanuel asked, finding himself again in the situation where he suspected and dreaded the answer.

"We never eat our own!"

"*Then how do you know they're good to eat?*"

"Toovall. Sometimes Kambe. But, the Toovall don't guard theirs as well..." The woman grinned, and her eyes glittered.

"Doesn't matter," a man broke in. "We'll take our revenge on the Kambe soon, even if they are better fighters."

OF COURSE, if the bovinid was finding eternal peace in sacred burial ground, Emmanuel could guess what was happening to the Kambe man. Eternal unrest in the fires of a cooking stove. And, later, in the burning acid of a village worth of stomachs. Emmanuel disengaged himself from the crowd. He needed a walk. To clear his head.

His plan hadn't worked. He wasn't a hero.

Why? These people had never seen animals before Emmanuel brought the bovinids and sheepalos. The only forms of life they knew were human and plant: the former being intelligent, soulful, busy, creative, and myriad in its ways; the latter being still, passive, and simple. This was especially true on a world that was pre-floral. There were towering conifers and brushy ferns, wind blown reeds and carpets of grass. From what Emmanuel had seen, that was about it.

When these tribal people looked into bovinid eyes, what did they see? Human, plant, or something new? Emmanuel expected them to see something new... Because he did. Something *in between*. But, no, when Alifia looked in Tiny's eyes, she saw intelligence, activity, and will. She saw a human soul.

Emmanuel put his hand to his head as if to ward off a headache. His walk had brought him back to the *Clemency*, and he leaned against her, feeling weak.

Would he go back for the feast? Could he attend the feast and abstain from the main course? Or would that be a horrible offense? Even if it weren't, could he bear it? Being so close to roasted human flesh... His stomach turned. He understood now why EMA had experts for dealing with foreign cultures.

Before Emmanuel made up his mind what to do, Alifia found him. Tiny trotted behind her.

"You're leaving again," she said, realizing it before he had himself. There was sadness in her voice. An acknowledgement of the moment that had slipped away from them.

"Tell your people I'm sorry I couldn't stay," he said to his beautiful cannibal, barely able to look at her.

"Yes," Alifia assented grimly, knowing there was something wrong but having no way to know what it was.

Emmanuel knelt down to ruffle the curly fleece on the fledgling sheepalo's head. Tiny pushed his head against the scritching fingers.

"Unless..." Alifia said the words suddenly: "Unless you'll take..." She broke off just as suddenly, but Emmanuel could hear the echo of the words she meant to say: *take me with you.* There had been hope in her voice, but she could see the 'no' in his eyes and entire demeanor; she could sense the finality of it. So, instead, she finished with the words, "...take Tiny with you. You should have a companion, and he likes you, I can tell."

Amused and relived, Emmanuel agreed to that and found little trouble convincing the beast to stay with him as they watched Alifia descend back into the woods. In his mind, he said his final goodbye to her, banishing her from his daydreams forever. She was too much for him.

He toyed with the idea of marching back to the village, standing in a pulpit, and explaining to the cannibals that their ancestors and the people of the Expansion considered cannibalism to be *wrong*. But he suspected it wouldn't do any good. Better to let the experts handle it. The EMA could reform them, even if Emmanuel could not.

Emmanuel led his new pet onto his ship and prepared the *Clemency* for takeoff. Tiny followed him around the ship, and eventually curled up at the base of the pilot's chair. As Emmanuel pulled his ignition key from his pocket and settled into the pilot's seat, he resolved to do the right thing and report the cannibals to the EMA as soon as he hit dock at the next space station.

He would be glad to get off this world and back to civilized space. A bovinid steak was sounding pretty good right about now, and he needed to pick up some cereal cookies for Tiny. Breath shook the downy belly of the sleeping beast; Emmanuel could feel the weight and warmth of the tiny body against his booted foot. He looked down at Tiny, and he thought about what he saw.

He tried to see a person in the fuzzy beast, but all he could see was a pet. He wouldn't even feel guilty eating a sheepalo burger while Tiny was on his ship. Maybe there was something special about a people who treated animals like equals. Emmanuel didn't know. Yet, as the Clemency zoomed away from the troubling world, Emmanuel decided to put off making his report to the EMA a little longer. In fact, the paperwork was sure to be a burden. Maybe he wouldn't make the report at all.

7

FOR THE SAKE OF MUSHROOMS

The red sun glowed like an evil eye on the forward viewscreen. It stared into Irudy's soul. Once it had been the warmth on her fur and the shine in a smiling sky while she ran through fields, her paws bare against the wholesome dirt. Now it was death's mocking wink, as the cold, stale air of her cargo ship recycled endlessly through algae filters and mechanical pipes.

Irudy steered her cargo ship, angling it into a languid orbit of the red giant, chasing slowly after the burnt rock that had once been her homeworld, before the cheerful yellow star called Heffe had betrayed her and her entire people. Over a single generation, the yellow star had been rushed into an early convalescence as a red giant by mad scientists trying to rejuvenate it. A whole race of sentient canids had scattered to the winds of space, their myriad cultures dissolving into treasured fragments and the half remembered legends of refugees.

On the star maps, the sun's name was still the same. But this red giant didn't deserve a name.

It didn't deserve to be remembered.

And yet Irudy felt called to it.

Again and again, she came here, swung past the dusty, scorched world that had once been a glittering green-and-blue gem, and then pointed the nose of her small vessel towards the sun.

Was she saying goodbye? Or was she telling the planet, I won't forget you? I'm coming home soon. The red giant swallowed your oceans and trees. Now it will swallow me.

In the belly of the red giant, could Irudy find her lost home? Red-furred canids had played chase and tag, running and laughing, barking and singing songs. All in the blink of a red giant's eye, that was gone.

Irudy could be gone too.

What was there to keep her? To pull her away from the red giant's gravity, back into the confusing universe that her people had been thrown into? A shipload of cargo. Mushrooms from two star-systems over that would spoil, if she didn't deliver them to Crossroads Station on time.

Except, they couldn't spoil in the belly of a sun. They'd be burnt to a crisp. Cooked to nothing.

A niggling, useless thought reminded Irudy that these type of mushroom weren't cooked with heat by the reptilian aliens who'd ordered them; they were brined. It didn't matter, and yet, somehow it was enough to make her point the nose of the cargo ship away from the sun, back on a course to Crossroads Station.

Irudy could always come back after the mushrooms were delivered. She could, and she probably would.

And yet, somehow, every time, there was some piece of cargo in her hold that had to be delivered. An artist's paintings, and the artist, a koala-like alien, had held Irudy's paws, squeezed them, and made her promise to be careful with them. Or replacement robot arms, and Irudy couldn't stand the idea of those poor robots missing their arms. Or something truly important, perhaps vaccines or a passenger who didn't understand why Irudy had flown off their flight path to visit an abandoned sun.

Or this time, mushrooms.

It wasn't a good reason to live.

But today, it was enough.

8

THE AMBI-COGNITIVE MAN

The starhopper had been parked on the edge of town for several hours. After the seven star jump to get all the way to Neggemmon, Jordy figured his friends would want to get right out and meet the natives, so to speak. He understood when Tom recommended fixing lunch first. (Seriously, you can never trust the food in out-of-touch Expansionist colonies. Forget a colony for long enough, and they'll start harvesting vacuum-slugs to eat.) But he started to get suspicious when Henry suggested relaxing with a quick hand of cards.

One quick hand stretched into several, and Henry kept heckling Tom into playing "just one more." To give him a chance to win his money back.

"I don't understand you guys," Jordy said. "I'd be as excited as hell to get out there, if I were you."

"You think we're not excited?" Henry looked calm and collected, completely focused on his cards. *Not* excited. When Henry looked up, he saw the raised eyebrow expressing skepticism in Jordy's face. "What?" he said. "This is my poker face. If I looked excited, it'd give away my hand."

"If you're so excited, why are we still playing cards?"

"Henry's afraid," Tom said. Henry cuffed Tom on the shoulder. Jordy could always trust one brother to rat the other one out. Though, looking them in the eyes, Jordy could tell that both of them were scared.

"Why are you two more afraid to go out there than I am? You'll fit right in. Everyone's going to stare at me."

Henry opened his mouth to answer, but Tom cut him off before he could make a sound. "Being stared at is our niche. Fitting in scares us." Henry nodded agreement and turned back to his cards.

Jordy let that answer sit and finished the hand. Afterwards, Tom and Henry shuffled the cards and began dealing them again, their two hands working together with the ease that years of practice brought.

Responding to an impatient look from Jordy, Tom said "Hey, I'm ready whenever. If you can convince Henry, that is." The brothers shot each other a meaningful glance. Jordy could tell it was meaningful, but he couldn't divine the meaning. It was twin code. "That's why I wanted to bring you, you know. To give Henry a kick in the pants when he chickened out. Just don't kick too hard." Tom grinned; he didn't have to add "*They're my pants, too.*"

Henry scowled. "That's not why we brought you." He bent his well-groomed head over the freshly dealt cards, carefully examining his fanned out hand.

It was the small things that reminded Jordy of Tom and Henry's strangeness—like the way Henry could deftly arrange his cards holding them with only one hand. Other people stared for the larger, more obvious, cruder reason: "Hey, look, there's a man with two heads!" Jordy could never think of them that way; more like two men sharing one body.

Tom and Henry were that rarity in a day and age when most children were genetically tweaked and hormonally toned by their parents: a child who was conceived naturally but who had come out unusual enough that he—*they*—couldn't hide it. Conjoined twins, with two legs, two arms, and two heads. If you weren't paying attention, they appeared to be normal, separate brothers, albeit sitting unusually close to each other, with their missing arms most likely around each other's backs. Still, if even their best friend couldn't help sometimes staring at them, then Jordy couldn't blame Tom for calling it their niche.

Henry looked up to see Jordy and Tom still watching him. "You haven't looked at your hands," he said. "Oh, bloody, all right." He threw his cards back down. "We can go."

The road into town was dusty, and the first buildings it passed were small and wooden. They were buildings that could be built by hand from the natural resources of the world. As such, they were the first hint of flavor to grace the senses of Jordy and his hesitant friends. Jordy saw nothing special about the buildings, but Henry noticed that the doors were unusually wide. He sometimes felt crowded by the doorframe when he and his brother walked, together, into a room. Wider doors was nice.

The three travelers continued down the rural road toward the center of town. They could see, looming before them, past the little wooden buildings, the cookie-cutter mansions found in any Expansionist colony from the first-wave. Back then, in the hurry to *Expand* with a capital *E*, the seeds of humanity were shot toward any and every likely star system like dande-lion fluff on the wind. The Expansionists tried generation ships, cryo-ships, natal-ships (loaded with fetuses to be birthed on arrival—a complete disaster), and anything else that crossed their star-craving minds.

Often, prep-convoys were sent ahead to ready the new colony for its coming inhabitants. They brought Earth-Zero plants, animals, terra-forming machines to tweak the atmosphere, and the unassembled, super-alloy buildings Tom, Henry, and Jordy were approaching now.

Only, sometimes, the prep-convoys were forgotten. And the rest of the colony never arrived.

Usually, forgotten colonies dwindled to nothing as the prep-pilots slowly died, leaving ghost towns on the invisible planets circling distant stars dotting the Expansionist sky. Sometimes, the prep-pilots forged on and started their own colonies from their limited genetic stock combined with genetic samples and records dragged along. Then strange things happened. Things like Neggemmon.

For all the strangeness, Jordy felt oddly at ease. Perhaps it was his reaction to Tom and Henry's skulking sullenness. They both seemed to feel it was the other's fault they were here. Neither made eye contact with the people they were beginning to pass, entering the town's thickness. Jordy, however, nodded greetings to the surprised onlookers. Double visages stared at him from every direction, but Jordy knew his place, so their eyes in fours didn't bother him.

Jordy had to keep Tom and Henry here until they loosened up, became themselves again, and got to know these people who must have more in common with them than anyone on Crossroads Station, planet Da Vinci, or even their homeworld. As long as Jordy continued to forge ahead, the brothers were forced to meekly follow him. After all, Jordy had pocketed the keys to the star-hopper.

"Let's find a bar," Jordy said. He expected no response from Tom or Henry so he spoke loudly. As hoped, two women nearby overheard him. They rushed toward him, shuffling on their two feet, overburdened by overweight. They were a plump woman.

"There's a good bar in New Town," the right sister said. "You're clearly new here..." She was looking Tom and Henry over as she spoke; the left sister smiled placidly.

"That sounds great," Jordy said, thumping Henry in the arm, since Henry was the closer brother. Back at Crossroads Station he was also the more social... He took the hint.

"I'm Henry," Henry said, putting out a hand to shake.

"And Tom," Tom added, putting out his hand.

The sisters looked confused, but they put out two hands, making a strange hand-holding hand-shake. "Nice to meet you..." the right sister, who was speaking, stumbled over their names, "*HenryandTom*. I'm Claire."

"And you?" Henry asked, locking eyes with the left sister.

Unnamed, the left sister glanced between the faces looking expectantly at her. She looked as though she wanted to hide. Henry inclined his head, further urging a response.

The right sister, perplexed, repeated "I'm Claire. *Claire*."

"Yes, but..." Tom began, sounding contentious.

Henry quickly interrupted, saying "It's nice to meet you, Claire."

Claire smiled, and her unnamed sister relaxed into anonymity.

"Yes, and I'm Jordy. Now, about that bar?"

"Would you like me to show you there?" Claire asked, but before any of them could answer, her unnamed left sister cut in. "Actually," unnamed said, "I have to get to the gravbuggy repair before it closes."

Claire murmured, "Yes, yes, I forgot. I can be so forgetful..."

The unnamed sister continued, "but I can give you directions." Unnamed spoke very precisely, verbally guiding them along the path they would take to the bar in New Town.

When she was done, Henry thanked her, and then he switched his gaze from the bashful left face to Claire's smiling face on the right. "And thank you, too," he added.

"Yes, we're very grateful." Tom stumbled over the words, clearly nervous, but he still smiled at each plump face in turn.

"You're an odd one," Claire said, squinching her eyebrows,

looking between Tom and Henry, trying to figure these strange off-worlders out. At last, she concluded, "You should meet my sister. She likes the odd ones."

All eyes—except Claire's—turned to the unnamed woman sharing Claire's lumpy shoulders, but her shy smile hadn't changed. Tom and Henry shared a glance out of the corners of their eyes, and Jordy tilted his head, trying to make Claire's statement fall into place.

"Yes, yes," Claire asserted, "you should definitely meet Lori." The unnamed woman spoke, as if in answer to Claire, "I can stop by Lori's office after I pick my gravbuggy up." Claire picked up right where unnamed left off, saying, "I'll send her your way. She would enjoy having a drink with you two."

At first, Jordy thought Claire meant Tom and Henry, but from the way she looked at him, he couldn't help feeling included in the "*two*."

The walk to the bar was quiet. Jordy was mulling over the conversation with Claire and her strangely quiet conjoined twin. Tom and Henry simply seemed shell-shocked by their new environment. Jordy couldn't blame them, though he wouldn't have guessed what they were thinking. Each brother was wondering, in his own way, whether they looked as strange as Claire and her twin did. Every day, Tom and Henry saw themselves in the mirror. They thought they were used to what a pair of conjoined twins looked like. Instead, they found that they were used to what *they* looked like. Since Claire and her twin didn't look like them—or like anyone else they'd met before—they looked... *odd*.

As the brothers walked through the wide-set door into the *Drowsy Apricot* bar, Henry finally managed to put the feeling bothering him into words: "How can I feel like Claire and her twin looked like a freak, when we look just like them?"

"Maybe they are a freak," Tom answered. "Who comes running up to talk to off-world strangers like that anyway? I could never be that chirpy. Besides, we don't look just like them."

Henry fell into silence as they approached the bar. It was made from a wood-grain patterned metal-alloy, and the shelves behind it were lined with bottles, decanters, glass mugs, and metal canteens. The bartenders, a pair of twins with stylishly shaggy hair, were polishing the faux wood with a dust rag. The left twin asked the arriving customers, "What can I getcha?"

Tom ordered a beer for himself and the *apricot special*, advertised on a flashing monitor behind the bar, for his brother. He knew Henry would want to sample the local special. Jordy waited to order while the bartenders worked together to whip up the fancy, mellow orange drink. When the apricot special was done, the left bartender slid it down the bar to where Jordy was sitting and said, with a wink, "Here ya go *brother*. Enjoy your special."

"No," Henry interjected, pulled from his reverie. "That's for me. Jordy isn't our brother. Just a friend." He grabbed his frothy orange drink, coordinated with Tom picking up his beer, and the brothers moved seamlessly to a nearby table. Tom liked sitting at the bar, but he knew from long experience that Henry would be miserable if he forced them to stay. He also knew that once Henry relaxed a little, at the privacy of their own table and with the help of a few drinks, they could probably move back to the bar. Tom would chat with the bartender then.

While Jordy ordered a drink for himself, Tom and Henry watched other customers wander through the wide front door. Most of them looked like regulars, with regular spots at the bar or tables. Two girls in particular caught Henry's eye, and he reached over to tap Tom on the wrist, making sure he noticed them too. They looked more out of place in the bar than the others, like they were looking for someone. More importantly, they were exactly Tom and Henry's type—cute bobbed hair and a snub nose, well, two snubbed noses, one on each of them.

"Now that's why we're here," Tom said, then took a gulp of his beer and raised the glass for the left sister to see as she passed them, heading toward the bar but looking back at him. He wanted to get up and follow her. He tensed his leg to stand, but he didn't feel any answering tension from Henry's half of the body. Tom sighed. There would be time later, when the apricot alcohol loosened Henry up... And, this way, the girl had more time to glance back at him over her shoulder, and maybe gossip about him with her twin.

Jordy joined them, setting his beer stein before him on the table. Jordy was still thinking about the spooky conversation they'd had with Claire. "Do you guys think there was something wrong with Claire?" he asked. He didn't mean *Claire*, exactly, but he couldn't bring himself to refer directly to her sister—she'd seemed more like a ghost, phantoming Claire than a real person like Tom or Henry.

Tom barely gave him a glance in response—still absorbed in watching the snub-nosed sisters, and Henry said "Claire? The girl we met on the way in?"

"Never mind," Jordy said. After a deep gulp of beer, he changed the subject, saying "So, why is this colony here?"

"Blind luck?" Henry suggested, beginning to relax into an apricoty haze. "Someone in the universe likes us." He looked sidewise at Tom, lifting the dregs of his fancy drink to clink glasses, but Tom disagreed.

"I've told you the history," Tom said, his attention snapping back to the table, away from the snub-nosed girls (who were indeed glancing, occasionally, over their shoulders at him). For history buffs like Tom, stories about generations dead girls can be more important than live girls two tables away. He began the story: "There were a pair of brilliant pilots—two sisters. Conjoined."

"Like us," Henry added, and, waving his glass around to indicate the entire room, "like them!"

Tom ignored him. "These sisters claimed that their success with long-range space missions had to do with their ability to work together and keep each other company in the dead of space."

"This was back during Wave-1 Expansion?" Jordy asked.

"Right, way back when," Tom said. "Anyway, the Expansionists thought these sisters, Lana and Elly Chang were right. So, they sponsored a fellowship program. If you wanted your kids to have a confirmed education and career before they were even born, all you had to do was sign on the dotted line, allow them to use a special hormone treatment in the womb at the right time and BAM. You've got twins. Well, sort of."

Henry snorted. "They targeted poor families, didn't they?"

"Well, that's not in the records. But it's a good bet."

"So..." Jordy began to put the pieces together. "The government trained all these conjoined twins to be pilots. Then, they sent them off to set up this colony."

"Right."

"I've heard crazier stories from back then. Did I tell you about the colony founded by a natal-ship?"

"Yes," Tom said. "I've heard about that one. Not enough nannies were sent along. Anyway... When, the conjoined pilots got here, to Neggemmon—only it was *Negemon*, with one 'G' and one 'M' back then—they were stranded."

"One of the abandoned prep-teams for whom the colony never shows up," Henry clarified, showing he was, despite his attempts to one-handedly build structures out of the coasters, paying attention.

"Except, unlike most of them," Jordy said, "this abandoned prep-team persevered."

"Yes," Tom agreed, "they decided to make a home for themselves here and have children. Only, they decided to make the next generation in their own image."

"In our own image!" The coasters fell over. Henry added, happily, "Cheers!"

Jordy and Tom caught each other's eyes, silently agreeing that one apricot special seemed to be enough. Tom would have liked another beer, but it wasn't worth the effect it would have on Henry. Even though they shared one bloodstream, Henry never could handle alcohol as well as Tom. Tom suspected it was a ploy—an excuse to let go and become the irresponsible one. But, he'd never caught Henry in the act, and he probably never would. So, it was better to play along.

"I think I'll head back to the bar and get some water," Tom said. He asked Henry, only half-joking, "Want to come along?" Since the brothers couldn't go anywhere without each other, they'd learned this pride-saving strategy long ago: inviting Henry to join him was better than asking Henry's permission to leave.

"Oh, sure," Henry said, shoving the coasters into a little pile. The two of them rose, and Tom drew a sharp breath when he saw the girls he'd earlier had his eye on watching him. The left sister smiled, and the right sister beckoned them over.

"Hello," Henry said, as they seated themselves beside the girls at the bar.

"Can we get some water?" Tom addressed the bar-tenders. The bar-tenders inexplicably looked at the girls, who shrugged, before nodding and grabbing two glasses. Filled to the brim, the waters sloshed as the bar-tender shoved them towards Tom.

"Thanks," the snub-nosed girl on the right said, taking one of the waters. "But, you're not going to impress a girl much with water."

"Actually..." Tom said, "that water was for me." He put his hand out, and carefully, tentatively took back his water. The girls complied, letting him have the water, but they were both giving him the funniest look. The left one said, her eyes flickering between the two brothers, "You *must* be the man my sister was talking about. Then, fluidly, the right one added: "My sister is Claire. I'm Lori." Back to the left: "You must be... *HenryandTom*." Her eyes never left Tom's face as she rushed both names together, chin held high and straight.

Her other head, for Tom had a terrible feeling that's what the beautiful face on the right was, tilted provocatively, waiting for his answer. It made her even cuter in his estimation than she'd been before. "Actually, *I'm* Tom. You're Lori?" he asked her.

"Yes," the left face smiled; the right one squinched her snub-nose adorably.

He tried again, looking directly into the eyes of the face on the right. "You're Lori?"

"Yes." In unison. Their lilting voices were both haunting and beautiful spoken together like that. A shout into a canyon, repeated to coincide perfectly, almost perfectly with its echo. Tom looked at the two faces—he saw two girls, sisters, deserving to be equals. Was one of them only a shadow?

"I don't know how to explain this," Tom said, tapping Henry's arm. Henry was slumped over his water, forehead leaning heavily into the heal of his hand. Tom desperately wished he would snap out of it; he could really use Henry's support. "I'm a little confused..." Henry was at least paying attention now, so Tom spoke to him. "This girl—these girls— they both say they're Lori."

"They've got the same name?" Henry asked. He clearly wasn't getting it.

"I don't think so."

Lori was watching them closely. "You came in with him?" Her left self twisted around and pointed at Jordy.

"Yes," Tom said.

"You're from off-world," she said. "All you've known is... *people*," there was a strange twist to the way she said the word, and Tom thought he saw her right self mouth the words *half-people*, "like him." It wasn't a question.

"Full ambi-cognitive schism," the right Lori said, staring somewhere between Tom and Henry's faces. Henry didn't know what that meant, but he knew it ruffled him the wrong way. "I've never seen a full blown case before." The left Lori was looking at them closely, noting their different reactions.

Tom tried to play it cool. "You're a psychologist or something?" It bothered him after he said the words that he didn't know which woman he was asking... He feared he was asking both of them, despite the singularity of his noun.

"Yes," Lori said with her left mouth and offered Tom her right hand. "It's an honor to meet you."

At least, that was how she saw it.

Even though the Lori who spoke—the brain in her left head —wasn't controlling the hand, couldn't feel the sensations in it when Tom cautiously took it in his rough hand, she felt complete ownership over it. Maybe her smile was less warm on her left face than on her right, and there was less of a blush from the feel of Tom's warm fingers, but that didn't make Lori feel any less like they'd shaken hands.

That's how it felt to shake hands for her.

Henry, on the other hand, only watched the handshake. He saw his brother take and hold the delicate, slender fingers of a beautiful woman. She might be saying strange and upsetting things, calling him names he didn't understand, and elusively refusing to identify herself (for it still hadn't sunk in for Henry that the sisters he saw were an illusion of his perspective and upbringing).

No, in Henry's eyes, Tom was making time with an annoying but beautiful girl, and she had a sister, sitting right there, next to her, waiting for him. A sister she wouldn't feel squeamish about sharing too much of her private life with... A sister he could kiss and make love to while Henry did the same with his girl. For Lori (and the phantom sister that Henry imagined when he saw her) it would be the same act of love in the same way it was for Henry and Tom.

"Hi, I'm Henry," Henry said. He stuck his hand out, hovering it hopefully near Lori's previously unshaken hand. Lori looked amused and a little confused in both her faces, but she lifted her hand from resting on the bar and placed it in his. Henry gripped it firmly, gently, before letting her slip her hand away. The blush and warmth reached her left cheeks now. It was subtle. Lori didn't understand the difference, but she knew the man—insane though he was by her culture's definition— had charmed her. She didn't know how; she didn't realize that his simple insistence on shaking hands with both of her hands made her two halves more equal, relevant, realized. *Whole.*

"And I'm Lori," her left self repeated. "I thought we were past the introductions," she was smiling, almost laughing as she spoke, "but I guess they're a lot more complicated if you have a dual identity."

"Hey!" Henry exclaimed. He sputtered before recovering himself enough to say, "Look, I'm trying to be nice here, and you keep throwing these names at me."

"Calm down, Henry," Tom said.

"Do you even know what she's talking about? Or her? You're making awful nice-nice with her, but I don't know what in the hell either of them is talking about."

Tom opened his mouth to speak, but Lori put her right hand on his right to stall him. "I'm sorry," she said. "I've never met someone like you." Her eyes on the left darted between both brothers, and she quickly added, with her left self, "Like either of you." Her right self picked up the hint and fluidly continued, "I should know better than to throw technical jargon around like that, but, you—" Her left self added, "—both of you—" Back to the right, "—need to understand that no one here has met anyone like the *two* of you."

After a pause and a nervous glance at the bartender, who was watching them skeptically, Lori's left self concluded: "It's likely to cause a lot of confusion."

The bartender snorted with one head and muttered, "To say the least," with the other.

"You want to keep out of this, buddy?" Henry asked, hostility dripping from every word.

"Henry..." Tom said, hoping to placate his brother. He could tell Henry's temper was sorely unbalanced, and he didn't want to end up in a fight. Though, the adrenaline in his blood, coursing through his body at an accelerated rate due to Henry's fear and anger racing heart wasn't making it easy for Tom to stay steady either.

The bartender put up his hands, palms out. "My mistake," he said. "Private conversation." He gestured with the rag he'd been using to wipe down the bar and looked at Lori, "I'll be over there if you need me, Lori."

Lori smiled, tight lips on both mouths, and was about to thank the bartender when Tom and Henry leapt from their seat. Tom had tried to stay stolidly seated, but Henry's fury had won the day. "That tears it," he yelled. "You think this crazy lady has anything to fear from me?"

"*Henry.*" Tom's voice sounded like their father's in his ears. He hoped it sounded that way in Henry's ears too. "You're making me look bad. You're making *yourself* look bad."

"Sounds to me like these people think that's the same thing."

"All the more reason for me to want you to sit down, Henry."

"Well, I don't have to care what you want."

While they spoke, Tom and Henry stood rooted in one spot. Tom had his hand on the bar and was trying to reseat themselves; Henry had his hand balled into a fist and was straining to leap toward the bartender.

Fortunately, the pique in Henry's voice called Jordy's attention. Before anyone else could react to Henry's rising tone, Jordy was across the room and had laid a staying hand on his shoulder. "You don't want to get in a fistfight," Jordy said. "You know you don't."

Henry relaxed a little, knowing what Jordy said was true; Tom breathed a sigh of relief.

"Why don't you two go back to the star-hopper? I can clear the tab here." Jordy pulled the keys out of his pocket and handed them to Tom.

"Thanks, Jordy," Tom said, meaning much more than *thanks for covering the tab*. He took a tentative step back from the bar, trying not to press his luck too hard too fast. After an awkward moment of holding that careful balance, Henry's foot followed suit. They were able to turn away together and walk for the door.

Once they were gone, the tension in the bar palpably lessened. However, it wasn't gone. Conjoined natives who had been keeping a pair of eyes on the worrisome newcomers still had one worrisome newcomer to watch. Jordy could tell he was subtly the center of attention, but he wasn't bothered by it like Henry had been. This wasn't his world, and he knew it never would be. So, he was free to ignore the opinions of him that he could feel forming around him.

He took a few credit chips out of his wallet and set them on the bar, moving closer to Lori in doing so. The bartender looked at the currency curiously. "Credit chips?" he asked.

"Yeah," Jordy answered. "They're good here, right?"

"I guess so..." the bartender said. "I mean, we did join the League... I've just never seen them before." Credit chips were the official currency of the League of Expansionary Planets, but most colonies used an unofficial local currency as well.

"Can I get another beer over here?" Jordy asked. "I think I'm gonna need it before joining up with my mates again." He spoke loudly on purpose, hoping to break the tension. It worked. The bartender's smile became easier, and Jordy heard a snort of a laugh from somewhere in the bar behind him.

The bartender slid Jordy's fresh beer along the bar top, froth slanting and spilling over the edge before it stopped almost in front of Lori. Jordy took the stool beside her, where Tom and Henry had been sitting before, and picked up the dripping beer. He sucked the foam off the top and tried to mop the sides down with a napkin. He was stalling, trying to figure out what to say to this pretty girl—*girls*, in his mind still, no matter what he'd figured out about how this colony worked—whom Tom and Henry clearly liked.

"They like you," he said.

"*Both* of them?" right-Lori asked. "And," from left-Lori, "all of *me*?"

Jordy smiled. "You're right," he admitted. "It's more like half and half."

Quietly, left-Lori said, "I thought so." Both faces were smiling. A warm and beautiful smile. Jordy could see what attracted Tom to them. "We're not used to seeing our separate halves as separate people. A few people do, but therapy almost always helps them learn to fit in."

"You're a therapist."

Lori shrugged her shoulders. It was one motion her two halves could perform seamlessly, requiring both sides to be complete, without easily dividing into what could be seen as two separate motions. "Something like that," she said. "Actually a psychologist. But I do therapy sometimes. It's not called for a lot."

She switched back and forth between her mouths as she spoke—one sentence from the right, the other from the left. But, Jordy was trying to tune that out. If she thought of herselves as one person, he thought he should try to do so too. It was respectful. And practical.

Building up two separate Lori's in his mind would only confuse him. That way madness lay. He'd seen Henry treading there. But who better to tread towards madness with than a therapist? Or even a psychologist.

"Tell you what," Jordy said. "Would you like to go on a date with my friends? Or do a therapy session for them? Or something?"

Lori laughed. In stereo, from two beautiful faces, it was quite enchanting. "I don't usually mix dates and therapy sessions."

"If I can get them to meet you somewhere tomorrow..."

"The schoolhouse," Lori suggested. "Two o'clock."

"That wasn't what I expected... but, okay. If I can get them to meet you at the schoolhouse tomorrow, call it what you want —date, therapy session, research, whatever—will you be there?"

"Why me?" Lori asked. "Your... *friends* seem to have some rather ambiguous feelings about me."

"No," Jordy said. "They have some ambiguous feelings about your culture. You they like. Henry wouldn't get so worked up over a girl he didn't like."

Jordy finished off his beer and pushed the glass to the bartender's side of the bar. "Besides," he said, standing up and checking his pockets for cash, "if anyone here has a chance to reach through the confusion and paranoia in Henry's skull..."; he put down enough cash to generously cover the tab; "...it'll be a therapist."

Lori smiled and said, "Tell Henry, I'll be looking forward to seeing him, if you think that will help."

Jordy spent his walk back to the starhopper trying to decide if it would help, and otherwise generally strategizing how to spin Tom and Henry's date with Lori. He didn't have much luck. Basically, as far as Jordy could figure, Tom would be up for the date no matter how he spun it. Henry, however, would probably be wedged so far into the starhopper that it would take crow-bars to pop him out.

Fortunately, when Jordy stepped out from under the starry sky of Neggemmon and into the artificial warmth and light of the starhopper, he found Tom dealing solitaire at the table. Henry's hand lay limp, and his head lolled forward. He was sound asleep. So, Jordy whispered the setup to Tom, leaving him with the problem of getting Henry out on a date with a girl who'd upset him almost to the point of starting a fistfight.

It turned out to be easier than either of them expected. Henry was decidedly meek when he awoke in the morning. Most likely, he was embarrassed by his behavior the night before.

So, Tom and Henry were sharp and ready, outside the schoolhouse, at ten 'til two o'clock. They tried to look incon-spicuous, but they felt awfully strange hanging around a schoolyard watching the children play. Nonetheless, it was fascinating watching so many twinned children play. They played just like normal children... Swinging on swings, spin-ning the merry-go-round, and climbing the jungle gym. But... They still looked strange. Tom was fascinated by it; Henry was a little ashamed. He felt he should be better than people who had always laughed at him—not just by not laughing, but by not sharing a single feeling that they ever felt. Yet, he couldn't rise above it, so he just looked away.

Lori arrived, saying "I'm glad you came."

"Yes, we *both* came," Henry said, immediately regretting the antagonism in his voice. "I'm sorry about last night."

"Forget about it," Lori said. "No harm done."

Jordy had told Tom and Henry to try ignoring which Lori spoke when they... *she* spoke, but neither brother could do it yet. They both saw a talkative right-Lori and a strangely silent left-Lori. Tom didn't mind. He liked right-Lori, and he was fine with a quiet left-Lori tagging along. Like Henry was tagging along. Henry, however, was still bothered by left-Lori's silence. It made him want to draw her out. So, every time he spoke, he looked Lori in her left eyes, only looking at Lori's right face while she was actually speaking, and barely even then. It began to make him feel like he and left-Lori shared a secret conspiracy, both inwardly laughing at their siblings as they spoke.

Of course, left-Lori didn't think of right-Lori as her sibling, but she felt the secret connection to Henry nonetheless. It was strange to be wooed by a man like this. Their dominant heads showing a preference for each other, and their submissive heads doing the same. Not that Henry could really be described as submissive... By all the definitions of her society, Tom and Henry were crazy. But... She loved being pulled into his—*their* —craziness.

While Lori flirted quietly with Henry, mostly using her left eyes and smile, she also explained to Tom why they were meeting at the schoolhouse. She'd checked to make sure it would be okay with the third grade teacher, because she thought watching the children would help Tom and Henry understand the people here better. While fully ambi-cognitive adults were rare and generally barely functional in this society —unlike Tom and Henry seemed to be—ambi-cognitive children were relatively common.

Most of them developed coping mechanisms or otherwise grew out of it, but, in third grade, an ambi-cognitive child would still be struggling. Quite transparently, probably. And, Ms. Trebling, the third grade teacher, assured Lori that she did have a strongly ambi-cognitive boy in her class this year. *Anton.*

"We're really going to stand in the back of this class and watch the kids?" Henry asked when he realized what Tom and Lori had been talking about.

"That's the plan," Lori said, speaking from her left mouth out of deference to Henry's clear preference for it. "Give it a try," on impulse, she reached out and squeezed Henry's hand, "I think it'll make me make more sense to you."

Henry was completely won over by the feel of her hand on his. "Okay, I'm game."

When the three of them—Tom, Henry, and Lori—filed into the back of her classroom, Ms. Trebling was teaching her class addition by carrying. Her dominant self was talking, explaining the numbers on the board; her submissive self wrote the numbers and, between times, kept an eye on the class. That was they way she'd done it for years.

Looking around the room, Tom and Henry could see that all the children were following the same model. One child—or one half child, rather—wrote, copying the writing on the board; the other half stared straight ahead, clearly listening. Occasionally a child would raise a hand. If it was the hand that had been writing, the child asked a question like: "Is that number under the three a seven or a two?" If it was the hand that had been idle—the listener's hand—the question was about Ms. Trebling's lecture.

Tom and Henry looked at each other. They were both disconcerted. "When do the other children..." Tom began, but he realized he'd have to rephrase his question and started over. "I mean, do they ever practice writing with their other hands?"

"A little," Lori whispered back. They were both being quiet out of respect for the class. "Writing with both hands can be a useful skill sometimes. However, we rarely write as well with the second hand."

Tom frowned. He tried to imagine not being able to write and having to rely on Henry to do all his writing for him. It was a frustrating prospect. Fortunately, Henry didn't seem to be thinking the same thoughts. After last night, Henry didn't need any more frustration.

Tom followed Henry's gaze and saw that he was watching a twin boy in the front row. Neither of the twin boy's hands was writing; the page on his desk was a blank sheet, and both his faces were listening intently to the teacher. Lori had already spotted the boy and was sure he was Anton.

"Now," Ms. Trebling said, picking up a sheaf of papers from her desk. "Hand around these exercise, and let's see if you can do problems like this on your own."

There were a lot of frowns and otherwise serious faces as the children started looking over the worksheets. Ms. Trebling, walking among the desks, looking at the empty worksheets said, "Don't forget to think out loud."

There was a sudden roar as children started saying things like, "If I write the eight here..." or "So, I'll put a tick mark there..." The roar softened when Ms. Trebling admonished, "But, quietly, of course."

"That's so strange..." Henry said, watching the children. "It's like 'think out loud' means 'give orders to your twin.'" He looked at Lori, squarely in her left face. "Don't you feel ordered around if... um... well..."

"Don't I feel ordered around when I say I'm going to do something with my other head, planning on using this head to do it?"

"Um... yeah." There was an awkward pause, then Henry said, "It sounds silly when you put it that way."

"No, no..." Lori said from her right mouth. "I was just thinking of the best way to answer you." Switching to her left face, which had held a ponderous expression and still spoke carefully: "It's not silly, Henry. That can be a very big problem for some people. I noticed you looking at that boy in the front row—the one who wasn't writing with either hand."

Henry glanced back at Anton and could see that Ms. Trebling was kneeling beside his front row desk now, talking to him. She was saying, "Anton, where are your notes?"

"I'm sorry," the boy muttered, averting his eyes. At the same time, with his other head, he said, "At least I was listening!" casting a sheepish smile the teacher's way.

"Don't double-talk," Ms. Trebling said.

"I'm sorry," the face with averted eyes muttered again. Anton's other face stopped just in time to avoid a double-talk apology. It left him with his mouth goofily open.

Lori leaned close to Henry and whispered for both him and Tom to hear, "Anton's ambi-cognitive. Neither head is strongly dominant over the other."

"Neither head..." Henry muttered. "You make it sound like they're not people..."

"On this world, *they*'re not," Lori answered. "He's a person. And he's deeply conflicted."

As if to demonstrate the point, an outburst from Anton's direction drew the attention of the entire room. "I hate writing! My hand gets tired!" Anton's more surly head roared. At the same time, he threw all the papers on his desk at Ms. Trebling and his own other self. His other head threw a hand up to block the papers.

"*Anton*," Ms. Trebling admonished, grabbing him by both wrists to halt any further altercation, "you have to write."

The surly Anton glanced furtively at his other head. "Then I want to write with my other hand." Anton's other face contorted into a look of fury only a child still feels free to openly express. Bizarrely, in this case, Anton was expressing that fury at himself. He spoke in even tones, barely containing his anger as he said: "I don't want to write with my other hand. I like it the way it is."

Ms. Trebling sighed. "Anton, don't look at yourself while you're talking. You know better than that." She slowly let go of his wrists while Anton unclenched his hands. By the time his arms were completely free of the teacher's restraint, he'd dropped them loosely at his sides. His shoulders slumped in defeat as Ms. Trebling picked up his pen and held it out before him. "You have to practice writing," she said. "You can practice with both hands if you like, alternating between them. But, one way or another, you need to keep writing. Now, take the pen from me." Ms. Trebling kept her eyes firmly locked on the eyes in both of Anton's faces. "Take the pen, Anton."

The head that had caused the outburst held her gaze. His other face was the first to look away, and his corresponding hand reached out to take the pen.

"I'm sorry, Ms. Trebling," Anton said. "Very sorry," he amended, smugly, with his other head. Ms. Trebling accepted their apology and, as she stepped away, the two faces didn't look at each other, not even a sly one-faced glance.

Tom shuddered.

"You okay?" Henry asked.

"Yeah," he said. "It's just so damn spooky."

Lori took Tom's hand and squeezed it. Henry, watching, couldn't tell if he was jealous of Tom or pleased: with this girl, affection for his brother was theoretically the same as affection for him. But Henry wasn't used to thinking that way. And he didn't completely buy it. You could like some parts of a person and dislike others. So, even if "Lori" thought of Tom and Henry as two parts of the same person, they—*she*—could still prefer one half to the other.

And, after the fit he'd thrown last night, Henry could completely understand Lori not liking him.

"Let's get out of here," Lori. "It'll be easier to talk outside." So, still holding Tom's hand, Lori turned away and led her different minded visitors out of Ms. Trebling's third grade classroom.

Outside, Lori's hand fell away, and the brothers found themselves following her, on equal footing, again. The three of them walked toward the playground and circled around the monkey bars, swing set, and other play structures a while before talking again.

"It doesn't seem right," Tom said. "That kid hates himself."

Lori wondered how long it had taken Tom to choose how to phrase his sentence—and then how much longer to come to peace with it. "Don't you and Henry ever fight?" she asked.

Tom was silent, but Henry laughed.

"That's right," Lori said. "I guess I know you do. How is that any different?"

"We work it out," Tom said. "We get over it."

"Anton will work it out and get over it too."

Tom looked skeptical.

"He's just a kid right now," Lori said. "By the time he's an adult, he'll be over all those fights. He'll have figured out how to work with himself, get along with himself..."

"Dominate himself," Henry offered.

"Anton? I doubt it. That kid looks like he'll always be at least a bit ambi-cognitive." Lori looked at Tom and Henry and could see they weren't buying it. "But that's not the point," she said. "Kids often don't like the rules they're told to live by. Brush your teeth. Fold your clothes. Eat your vegetables. Just because *one* kid," the emphasis she put on the word sounded angry, almost hostile, "isn't happy, that doesn't mean the entire philosophy is wrong."

"If the philosophy's not wrong, then I want to hear that you're happy," Tom said.

"I'm happy."

"No," Tom said. "I want to hear you say it with each mouth. I want to hear each mouth explain how happy you are."

Lori looked taken aback. Each of her mouths was held a little open—wanting to speak, but not being ready to jump through the hoop Tom had held out for her. She grabbed the chains to one of the swings they were passing and stopped. She stood there. After playing with the links a minute, she sat down on the swing and looked at her feet pawing the bark dust ground beneath her.

Tom was watching her, but Henry was watching Tom. With a subtle rebalancing, from toe to heel, Henry started the two of them backing away. He wanted a word alone with his brother. So, the two of them made a quiet circuit of the playground together, leaving the Loris on her swing.

"What're you doing?" Henry asked, once they were out of earshot. "We have a real chance with this girl. She's not like any girls we've ever known before."

"That's because she's a domineering tyrant and a pathologically repressed and oppressed twin."

"Funny," Henry said. "Last night you were the one who liked her."

"As I recall you were about ready to punch the bartender out because you were so mad at *Lori*."

"Well, I guess I got it out of my system. Now it's time to get it out of yours. You really spark with that domineering tyrant, and I don't think I've ever met a sweeter girl than pathologically oppressed Lori. So what if they have the same name and some weird quirks about how to use pronouns."

"So, what're you saying?" Tom asked, looking back at Lori. He could only see her from behind, but he could tell that the dominant Lori was still watching her feet, and the submissive Lori was staring at the sky. "You'll take the quiet one, and I take the chatty one? Treat them like the sisters we know they are... even though they think they are not?"

"Yeah. Why not?"

"She thinks we're crazy."

"I don't have a problem with that."

"I do," Tom said. "We get along fine. You and me. And I don't want anyone, any therapists—even if they're pretty girls—messing with that. I don't want her trying to make me become submissive to you."

"Tom," Henry said. "If one of us were dominant, it'd be you."

"Whatever," Tom said. "I don't want her trying to *cure* us."

Henry couldn't argue with that.

The brothers continued to talk as they made another few circuits of the small play yard. They were trying to decide if this crazy colony held anything for them. Could they live with people they thought were crazy?

Yes. The answer they agreed on was *yes*.

And they could live with people who thought they were crazy too. But, they couldn't live with anyone trying to change them. Deny their separateness. Deny either of their personhoods.

"I don't think Lori wants to do that," Henry argued.

"How can you be sure?" Tom asked. "She's said we're crazy by her society's standards. And she's been defending her society's standards to us. What makes you think she sees any value in us the way that we are?"

And Henry couldn't answer that. So, they finished their current circuit. Quietly. At deadlock. And, when they came around the swing set again, they sat on the swing beside Lori. Tom stared into the distance. Henry looked down at their feet.

"Do you get lonely? Lori asked.

Tom looked over too slowly to see which Lori had spoken, but Henry looked up in time to see that it was the dominant one. The one who sparked with Tom. So, Henry held his tongue, shared a smile with Lori's quieter half, and waited with her for Tom to answer.

"I guess so," Tom said. "I mean, who doesn't?"

"I don't mean for a girl," Lori said. "I mean... really lonely."

"I guess not." Tom looked at Henry. "I've always got this guy to talk to."

Henry smiled at Tom, but then he went back to looking at the quiet Lori. "You get lonely," he said to her. "Don't you."

"Yeah," the quiet Lori said. Her dominant self agreed, "I do get lonely. I read," she said, switching back to her quieter side, "that was why we... the first colonists were like this... So, they wouldn't get lonely in the quiet of space." After a moment, her dominant self said, softly, "I never understood that. Until now."

"Until meeting you."

Both Loris were looking at Tom. She could tell that he was the one to win over now. He was the one who still had reservations. "Stay here," she said. "I want to get to know you. Both of you."

"All of me does."

Tom was quiet for a while. Then he asked, "When you get lonely, why don't you..." he paused, considering his words, trying to remember the words the third grade teacher had used, "...*think out loud*?"

"I do sometimes," the quiet Lori said. Her dominant self added, "But not much. We're trained not to." "That's what you were watching in that classroom."

"I figured," Henry said.

"Does it make you feel crazy?" Tom asked.

"Yeah."

"Do Henry and I seem crazy to you?"

"You should." "But no." "Not so much." "And, yet... Sort of." "In a good way." Her smiles were dazzling. Both Tom and Henry thought so, but Henry was the one who started them moving in to kiss her. The brothers' swing swung around, moving Tom, Henry, and the Loris face to face. Henry, being the right brother, faced the quieter, left-Lori. And, as he and she kissed, she found herself, on her right side, right in front of Tom. She initiated that kiss.

When the mess of them began to pull away from each other, Henry risked a quick peck on Loris right mouth. He wasn't sure what kissing both of her faces meant, but it made him giddy. And, Tom couldn't have minded too much, because he was the one to invite Lori to meet them for dinner that night. And, he didn't mention it on their walk back to the star-hopper.

On the way back, Henry kept rattling on about how great Lori was, and asking whether Tom didn't feel the same. But all his questions worked as rhetorical, and Tom let them stay that way. Henry wasn't worried. He could feel the swagger in Tom's stride; out of the corner of his eye, he could see Tom smiling; and, he could hear Tom's tuneless but happy hum.

Jordy was waiting for them in the star-hopper, cheating at solitaire. When he saw his friends walk in, Jordy said, "So, are we staying?"

"Yeah," Henry said, a grin spread across his face.

"Then, I guess it went well with Lori?" Jordy asked.

"Yes," Henry said, then looked sidewise at Tom, who added, "We're crazy about her."

9

THE GIRL WHO COULD HEAR THE STARS SING

It was so beautiful that the weight of it made her feel weak inside. She cried, and no one knew why. No one else could hear the music. But Brianna could hear it inside.

Brianna's parents didn't understand. They thought their child simply had an artistic sensitive soul, and perhaps, she was unusually susceptible to sunstroke. They tried to keep her inside on sunny days, especially in the middle of the summer. But Brianna craved the sun. It made her cry, but it also made her giggly and manic. Sunlight could make her happier than anything else—that voice whispering in her heart, rising and falling, raising expectations, holding out a moment longer than she thought she could stand, and then resolving. The music Brianna heard was the fabric of her life.

It was a constant battle between Brianna and her parents to keep her out of the sun. Her parents dressed her in long sleeves, turtlenecks, and unfashionable hats. When it got too hot for that, they slathered her in sunscreen. Brianna insisted that she didn't need protection any more than anyone else, but her manic tears when the sunlight hit her skin scared her parents more than a small child's clumsily chosen words could persuade.

So, Brianna learned to hide her feelings and let the music flutter inside her secretly. Until she learned to write.

As soon as Brianna figured out how to capture and codify music on her computer, around the age of nine, she disappeared from the world. Her parents were busy with her younger siblings by then—a toddler and a new baby—and were proud that their daughter could keep herself busy, especially in such a productive way.

Brianna shared only snatches of her music with her family. As she got older, she'd offer the occasional short composition for extra credit in an art class at school, and her teachers were always encouraging. However, the growing folder of music files on Brianna's computer might have stayed a personal treasure trove, a private solace untouched by the world, if her father hadn't convinced his sister to move home to Earth XI from planet Da Vinci. She brought her own family with her, including Brianna's cousin.

Michaela was a year older than Brianna, making the two of them closer in age than Brianna was to either of her younger sisters. They immediately became best friends. Cousins and friends is one of the best types of relationships that can exist, when it works out well. Cousins are not quite as close as siblings, so not in competition for attention from the same parents, but more closely bound to each other than friends who don't share overlapping family ties.

Michaela was more normal, more social than Brianna, and she soon drew her cousin out of the shell she'd built for herself out of the music from the sun. Michaela delighted in Brianna's compositions, and the two of them found ways to sing those celestial songs together, bringing them down from the sky and translating them into human, biological, earthly voices. The power and mystery of their celestial origin, though, remained infused, inextricably embedded in the melodies.

The two girls, singing together, could bring any audience—family, friends, even other kids at school—to tears with their haunting, joyous, unearthly songs. For by the time Michaela and Brianna sang the songs together, they were no longer merely the voice of a star. The two girls left their stamp on the celestial music. First Brianna had to simplify and codify the complex, intertwining melodies she heard, for a star is such a large creature, it can sing of many sensations, many feelings at once. Brianna's work with the music was always to simplify it. Then Michaela added words.

Brianna wasn't used to thinking in words; her world, her mind had been filled with the overwhelmingly large voice of a star for her entire life, and stars don't think or sing in words we recognize. She could make sense of the feelings, maybe, sometimes, but they didn't exist as words for Brianna. They existed as sounds, feelings, pure, untouched by human ideas. Michaela, however, took Brianna's simplified versions of the star's songs and fit pleasant, lilting lyrics to them. She had a knack for rhyming and clever turns of phrase. Occasionally, Brianna found herself frustrated with Michaela's lyrics, as sometimes they changed the nature of a song as she'd originally heard it.

When a star's feelings—gigantic and stretched over centuries—get condensed down to petty human understanding, something is necessarily lost. But something else is gained, and even as Brianna found herself frustrated by Michaela messing with the star's songs, she also recognized how much their parents—and their parents' friends, and any other adults they sang for—loved the little human stories that Michaela plastered over the surface of her star's deep, profound feelings. For she did think of Soliri—the yellow star that Earth XI orbited—as her star. She was the only person, as far as she knew, who could hear it.

Their music was a true collaboration. But only Brianna knew it was a collaboration between three—an ancient yellow star, a little girl who could hear the star, and a little girl who happened to be good at writing poetry. Occasionally, Brianna felt a fraud, watching Michaela write her lyrics from scratch. The melodies might be what made their music extra special, extra haunting—worldly beyond the years of two teenaged girls—but Brianna knew that she didn't write it by herself. She had a muse, and without the muse, she didn't know if she could write music at all. She needed Soliri. The star's voice had been her invisible, imaginary friend her whole life long.

As the girls got older, so did Brianna's younger siblings— Denise and Carla. As soon as they were old enough, Brianna recruited them to what had become her and Michaela's band— The Star Girls. Their voices were similar enough to Brianna's that their vocals blended together into harmonies almost as celestial as the ones that streamed down from the sky with the golden yellow starlight. The four-girl band became a world-wide hit before the first one of them reached the age of twenty.

Their fame spread beyond the Soliri star-system, and as soon as Brianna's youngest sister, Carla, was old enough to travel without their parents' chaperoning her, Michaela arranged for The Star Girls to go on tour. She reached out to asteroid amphitheaters and concert halls on faraway worlds, in different star systems. She arranged the entire tour. And then she told Brianna about it.

Brianna was struck with terror to her core. How could she leave Soliri? How could she fly on a spaceship through the darkness between stars? She wouldn't be able to hear the voice that had sung to her from before she could even remember. The voice that had been more constant, more soothing, more essential than even her mother's. She couldn't. She couldn't leave that voice behind.

But Michaela, Denise, and Carla were so excited about the idea of touring all the neighboring star systems, and the payments they'd been promised for performing were—excuse the pun—astronomical. Neither her sisters nor cousin would stand for Brianna shutting the idea of the tour down, and so she tried to toughen herself up. She prepared herself to hear silence, a lack of sound so deafening that she would be lost, abandoned and bereft. She felt terror, but she did her best to hide it.

And then the day of the first interstellar flight came.

Brianna had packed long-sleeved turtle necks, long pants, and layers upon layers of sweaters. She hoped to trick herself— bundle herself up so tightly that the pressure against her skin would trick herself somehow into believing the sun's songs simply couldn't reach her through the fabric.

Brianna paced the viewing deck of the space trawler that Michaela had booked passage for them on. She couldn't hear the sun's songs as loudly as she was used to, but then, the sun had always grown quieter at night, when the bulk of an entire planet blocked it from singing to her. She tried to hum along with the soft fragments of song that still ebbed and flowed along the corners of her brain like a low tide when the ocean pulls away from the shore.

Brianna kept her eyes on the star-studded darkness outside the ship's wide windows, hoping that if she could see the stars —even if they weren't her star, the sun that had sung to her for as long as she could remember—that her mind wouldn't fall totally silent. Michaela and her younger sisters teased her about her nervousness, and she tried to laugh it off, pretending she was simply afraid of the upcoming hyperspace jump.

And she was afraid. Deathly afraid.

When the space trawler jumped to hyperspace, the stars in

its windows stretched and spread like speckles of cream smeared across rich, dark gingerbread.

And the sound in Brianna's head distorted, skewing and slowing, dropping away. She wanted to scream, but she didn't. She clapped her hands over her ears, but she'd never heard the sun's singing with her ears. It had been deeper, all the way through her, filling every part of her with its resonance.

And now...

...the music was gone.

Brianna dropped to her knees, still clasping the sides of her head, wanting to tear her empty ears away. Her sisters ran to her, cajoled her, trying to pull her from the viewing room back to their own shared quarters, trying to avoid the embarrassment of whatever scene this was that their sister and bandmate was trying to cause. But Brianna shook them away. She stared through the window, staring as hard as she could at the stars streaking by in the distance.

And slowly...

...ever so slowly...

...she started to hear their voices.

Other voices, from other stars, that had been singing all this time, but she'd never been able to hear them.

Her own star, Soliri, had sung too loudly for her to hear these more distant voices over it. But now...

...oh my goodness...

...oh my stars...

There were so many voices, joining together, coming apart, harmonizing, and sometimes purposely fighting each other with discordant chords. There were stars that had held grudges against each other—singing out their war songs, while people lived on the planets that circled them, totally oblivious—for thousands and thousands of years, enough time for entire civilizations to rise and fall. Other stars sang to each other of loves so great they could wash over a minuscule human's life like it was a single grain of sand and the love was ten thousand thundering oceans, forty thousand blustering rain storms, and countless creeks, rivulets, and rivers. An entire ecosystem, all in a fragment of song.

Brianna's face, wet from tears, broke into a smile. Her smile—this one moment of relief and joy—was such a small thing compared to the feelings of a single star, and Brianna could hear them all. Well, maybe not them all. But so, so many stars.

Brianna's sisters and cousins were relieved when she seemed to get over her fear of space travel, but new conflicts arose. Now that Brianna could hear more music than she'd ever heard before, more different songs, she felt compelled to write them down, to capture as much of the celestial music as her ears, mind, and hands could convert to notation on a page. Michaela wrote words to match the new melodies, but she also complained: the new songs were different than the sound that had helped The Star Girls rise to fame.

Wouldn't it be better to write the same sorts of songs? The music they were known for? The music their fans expected?

But Brianna could only write what she heard, and Michaela had dragged her away from Soliri.

Regardless of the artistic tension between Brianna and Michaela, their tour mostly went well. They played to sold-out amphitheaters and concert halls. Entire asteroids rocked with the rhythm of their songs. Denise and Carla basked in the attention of their fans, and Michaela threw herself even harder into writing lyrics for the new music Brianna seemingly composed. When they were onstage, with massive crowds of all kinds of aliens cheering them, Brianna's sisters and cousins practically glowed. They danced; they twirled; they waved their arms at the crowds and beamed as the crowds threw their arms, tentacles, wings, and whatnot into the air and roared back their approval in response.

But Brianna felt alone. Among all the fans she'd met, not

one of them seemed to understand the deeper meaning of her music. Not once did anyone guess that the melodies came not from her, but were only channeled through her, streaming into her from the starlight that filled even the darkest corners of the galaxy.

Brianna began to consider giving her tenure as a musician up. She would always hear the music—she didn't know how to stop that, even if she'd wanted to. And she didn't want to. She loved the way that the conversations of celestial bodies filled her life, buoying her up, reminding her how small and fleeting every moment can be. You have to treasure them. A human life is but a blink of an eye to the life of a planet, and the life of a planet is, at best, a short-lived companion to a star, like dogs and cats are to us.

But those moments are all we have.

Yet, why write the music down?

Why share it with audiences who didn't understand?

Brianna could let the music wash over her, let it stream through her fingers like the water of a river, playing against her skin, cool and refreshing, bright and exciting, but always gone as soon as you feel it, always moving.

She had almost sworn to leave The Star Girls, a promise she kept secret to herself, when they came to the last star-system on their tour.

Denise and Carla were already scheming about how soon their next tour might be, and Michaela had finally accepted Brianna's new and changing styles of music. But Brianna simply didn't see the point of sharing music with people who clearly didn't understand it, listeners who were mostly interested in her cousin's trite lyrics. She planned to tell the others of her departure from the band at the end of their final concert.

Then she stepped out on stage, prepared to sing in harmony with her sisters and cousin. The audience looked different from any audience she'd seen before. Among the various mammals, avians, insectoids, and reptiles, there were clusters of creatures she didn't understand. They burned with a light of their own. They swayed as she sang, matching the deeper, slower rhythms of her songs, rather than the bouncy, catchier rhythms that Michaela had laid atop them.

Brianna peered into the audience, trying to understand what she was seeing. She didn't understand, but she could tell: it was important.

The dancing, swaying figures who burned like fires changed color over the course of the concert, glowing different colors for different songs. It almost seemed to Brianna that they matched their colors to the colors of the stars who had inspired different melodies. White for white dwarfs; red for red giants; blue for the one lovelorn ballad inspired by a blue super giant; and yellow—comfortable, familiar yellow—for the songs inspired by her own home-star, Soliri.

As soon as the concert ended—Brianna couldn't wait—she climbed straight down from the stage into the crowd. She pressed her way past delirious fans of all species, until she made it to the closest cluster of the aliens who burned.

"Who are you?" Brianna asked, not caring if the question was impertinent and tactless. She had to know. She had a connection with the people, some way, somehow, even if she didn't know yet exactly what it was.

With some translation help from some of the more humanoid members of the audience around them, Brianna was able to learn about these strange, alien people.

Strange and alien... except, at a deep level, they understood her better than anyone she'd ever met before, even her own cousin and writing partner who had shared everything with her for years. Almost everything. For Michaela couldn't hear the music of the stars.

The Flaenos were native to the current star-system—a

binary system with two white dwarfs—and like Brianna, they could hear the music of the stars.

"We live among the clouds of a gas giant—" one of the Flaenos explained, pointing towards the sky above the amphitheater's atmo-dome. The gas giant was too far away to look like anything but a star, but Brianna knew it wasn't one. It didn't sing. "—and we hear the conversation between our stars, waxing, waning, which one sings more loudly, but always singing to each other."

"Yes!" Brianna agreed. "I can hear them too." She'd heard the two white dwarves singing of their love for each other since long before the space trawler they traveled on had entered this star-system. Their love was strong; their shared song was lovely.

"But until your music—" The Flaenos's flames shimmered, shivering with the intensity of its feelings. "—we did not know other stars sang too."

Of course, the Flaenos had never heard other stars sing, since they couldn't spend much time on other species' space-ships, being so physiologically different, and they hadn't invented interstellar spaceships of their own yet. They'd felt no call to leave the singing of their own binary stars, singing that was loud enough to drown out all the more distant stars, just as Soliri had drowned out more distant celestial voices for Brianna until she'd left on tour.

Another Flaenos joined in, speaking faster than the reptilian alien who'd been translating could follow. Soon, Brianna was surrounded by living flames, each encased in a transparent spacesuit that kept its fire safely ensconced in its natural atmosphere. They poured their hearts out to her, as well as they could given that they didn't speak Solanese and Brianna didn't speak Flaenish. But they shared a deeper language. The language of the stars.

Brianna stayed at the amphitheater all night, and she convinced her siblings and cousins to go with her, the next day, to the Flaenos' gas giant. She couldn't visit their world exactly; she couldn't breathe its atmosphere or withstand its crushing pressures. But the Flaenos had a small space station in orbit that they used for interacting with other species. Many of them of came to meet her. Brianna realized her music had touched an entire world. And yes, she knew her music had meant something to other listeners as well... But it hadn't meant the same thing to those listeners as it meant to her. She didn't feel a connection through her music with them. It felt hollow. And she'd been ready to give up, leaving music behind.

Hearing the Flaenos tell her about how much it meant to them to hear the voices of other stars reflected in the music Brianna wrote down, unmarred by the lyrics Michaela laid on top... It meant everything to Brianna.

Brianna decided not to give up on her music. The stars' music. If the stars had chosen her—somehow—to be their scribe, then it was not for her to turn the role down.

The Star Girls finished their tour and returned home to the star-system of Soliri where the sunlight felt like a child's lullaby to Brianna. Pleasant, safe, and deeply comforting. But her mind was filled with the melodies she'd heard as they traveled, and she had much work to do, writing it all down.

10

LITTLE SANDY STARSTRONG AND
HER FAITHFUL ROBOT DOGS

"I told you not to feed the dogs scrap metal!" Sandy's dad said.

TJ coughed a telltale cloud of non-ferrous impurities, and L2D2 was still dulling his shiny alloy teeth on a ragged piece of scrap in the corner.

"They're just robots," Sandy said scowling. She kicked another piece of rusty pipe to TJ.

"I'll remember that next time TJ gets stuck in a command loop, and you come crying to me to fix her," her dad answered. He went back to programming their spaceship's flight plan. But then he stopped, and, after a moment's thought, said, "Actually, that's not a bad idea. It's time you took on more responsibility. I think you're old enough to repair your dogs yourself now."

Sandy groaned. "Can I go play?" she asked.

"Sure," her dad answered, without looking up from the spaceship console. They'd been on this asteroid a week, and he hadn't left the ship yet. Sandy had already found all the good playgrounds in the atmo-bubble community and made friends with the local kids. But she could sympathize with her dad. What was the point of making friends? They'd just be off to another asteroid next week when Mom finished teaching her seminar on robo-econo-ethics. Then Sandy would be alone again.

Of course, she had her dogs. They weren't real, but they were something. Sandy took them everywhere with her.

No matter how far she strayed from the ship, L2D2 could always lead her back home, and no matter how scary some of the asteroids they visited seemed, she could count on TJ to protect her. Only a fool would attack a little girl guarded by a model 6500 Roboweiler. The laser eyes could burn through metal in seconds, let alone hostile flesh. Not to mention the 6500's sonic attacks...

Little Sandy Starstrong was a very lucky girl to have two top of the line, all extras included, brains loaded with elasti-particle wiring, robotic dogs. Sure, at night they recharged on the floor beside her bed instead of snuggling with her, but then their plasti-alloy casings weren't all that snuggly anyway. And L2D2's glowing nose made an excellent nightlight. Sandy found it very comforting.

Today, Sandy headed for Kite Hill, a park where artificial anti-grav waves painted the sky. Of course, the painting they made stayed invisible until someone flew a kite—zipping and zagging through the high and low grav fields—through it. Sandy didn't have a kite, but she found it hilarious to watch TJ chase an erratic frisbee, hopelessly trying to predict where the fluctuating grav fields would ricochet it next.

Sandy wasn't the only kid to think of using Kite Hill that way, and when they got there, another dog was already running frantically back and forth to the hilarity of a boy about her age. There was something different about his dog though.

Sandy pulled an Aero-Supreme cybernetic frisbee out of her backpack and joined in the fun. She knew the boy, and they naturally fell into a rhythm, alternating their frisbee tosses to maximally spaz out their dogs. One frisbee after another—red

Aero-Supreme followed by the boy's yellow WindTronics—arched and looped above Kite Hill, and the dogs chased them as if their entire AIs were only subroutines inside an overriding loop, "IF Frisbee, THEN Fetch!"

Of course, all AIs are not created equal, and TJ clearly had the best frisbee tracking subroutines. L2D2 mostly ended up running around in little circles. The boy's dog, however, made up for any lack in spatially extrapolative algorithms with a natural grace that took Sandy's breath away.

When the game finally ended, dogs panting and L2D2's thermal meter reading dangerously into the red, everyone collapsed on the spongy Altarian moss covering the hillside.

"Jimothy?" Sandy asked, looking at the luxuriously fuzzy casing on his dog, "Where did you get your dog?" The eyes looked so real and bright.

"Oh, I've had him since he was a puppy," Jimothy said, patting the golden, floppy-eared head.

Sandy was trying to figure out if *puppy* was a brand or a model—clearly Jimothy had given the dog some serious upgrades, a complete overhaul—when she finally understood. "Oh," she said. *The soft fur, the pink tongue, the bright, liquid eyes...* She should have known. "I've never seen a real dog before."

"You thought Lucky was a robot?" Jimothy asked, and laughed. He gave his dog a hug. "You really do spend all your time on that spaceship!"

Sandy's cheeks reddened, but she was too mesmerized by Lucky to feel her embarrassment long. All she wanted was to reach out and touch that soft golden fur... "May I?" she asked, and received permission. The fur was coarser than she expected, but she could feel Lucky breathing beneath her hand. Not simulated panting, but real, warm breath.

TJ growled possessively, a mechanical whine, but it was too late. Completely enchanted, Sandy was in love.

She rushed back to the ship, and her first words to her dad, who hadn't moved, were "*I want a dog!*"

"You have two," he said, without looking up.

"Not a robot!" she countered, "a *dog.*"

Her dad frowned, and her mom frowned too when she got home. All they heard the rest of the week was *real dog, real dog, real dog!* And when they left for the next asteroid, Sandy sulked, alone in her room with poor TJ and L2D2 moping outside her door. The entire flight, her parents worried. Usually, Sandy spent flights between asteroids mourning the briefly known friends she'd left behind and anticipating the new friends she'd soon make. This flight, however, friends found no space in a mind dominated by *real dog.*

"Will you take care of it?" her mom asked when Sandy finally came out. (Sandy couldn't resist exploring a new atmo-bubble world, even to make a point to her parents as important as how much she wanted a dog.)

"Yes!" she cried.

"Real dogs eat real food, and if you don't feed them, they get hungry," her mom admonished.

Sandy rolled her eyes. Everyone knew that. Even so, she had to nod her way through a lecture about the time she let L2D2s battery run down, and she tried to recharge him with jumper cables and a friend's gravity-scooter. It hadn't gone well. Her dad had to special order a replacement alternator and spend several hours fixing L2D2 up in the shop.

Nonetheless, little Sandy Starstrong was a *very* lucky girl, and her parents decided to buy her a real dog. Sparky was a lanky, gangly spaniel at the tail end of puppyhood. His ears were curly brown, and the short, white fur on his body was covered in spots. Sandy lit up the moment she saw him, and he stole her heart when his wet tongue licked her face. There was no doubt; he was the one.

Her mom signed Sandy and Sparky up for obedience

classes, and her dad went with them. He wanted to be sure that Sandy *trained* Sparky, in addition to spending quality time with him. Of course, it turned out that—just as her mom had warned—training a real dog was hard work. Sparky didn't come preloaded with fetch, tag, hide-n-seek, and scramball. Nor could she simply hook him up to TJ and download those programs like she had with L2D2.

In fact, when Sandy wanted to spend the afternoon researching dog training on her computer, Sparky spent the whole time whining at her feet. He wouldn't leave her alone and wait quietly like she expected. Instead, he stared her down with sad eyes until she felt too guilty to concentrate.

So, Sandy leashed up Sparky for a walk and headed out. But Sparky kept tugging on the leash. Every time he saw a scrubber-bot, he'd dash toward it, yanking her arm this way and that until she couldn't take it any more. There was a park right at the edge of the space port—it looked like an abandoned cargo hold that had been painted to resemble a scramball court. Sparky took off running, as soon as Sandy let him off-leash.

He ran straight to a girl on the opposite side of the court. Sandy recognized Kella from Sparky's obedience class. "Where's your dog?" Sandy asked.

"Jellybean's not my dog." Kella picked up a nearby scramball and threw it for Sparky. "She's a police dog. My dad's letting me help train her, but she has to work. Like him. And Mom."

"Oh," Sandy said not knowing what else to say to Kella's obvious loneliness. "Aren't there other kids to play with?"

"Not a lot of humans." Sparky brought the ball back, but instead of dropping it, he danced around playing keep away. Kella grabbed him by the collar and pulled the scramball out of his mouth. A few fakes and one good throw sent him scrambling after it. Kella smiled. Then, she shrugged. "We only moved here a year ago, so... Yeah. I don't speak Altarian very well yet."

Sandy knew Kella seemed sad, but she couldn't help being jealous at the idea of living in one place for a whole year. Sandy could hardly imagine that. If she lived here for a whole year, she could be friends with Kella. Real friends, not the temporary kind.

While Sandy thought about it, she watched Kella play with Sparky. With surprise, she realized Sparky was actually playing fetch. He dropped the ball at Kella's feet, waited patiently for her to throw it again, and everything! "Hey," Sandy said, "you're good with dogs."

"Thanks," Kella answered, giving another throw.

"I'm not sure I'm cut out for it," Sandy said, sadly. She wondered if Kella would be a better owner for Sparky than her. "I never had to train my other dogs."

"You have other dogs?" Kella asked with interest.

"Just TJ and L2D2."

Kella still looked really interested.

"They're just robots," Sandy said, kicking at the ground.

But Kella's eyes grew wide. "You have robot dogs? No way! Where are they?" She looked around wildly, as if she thought they might have invisibility shields and have been playing fetch with her and Sparky all along. Which was of course ridiculous. Invisibility shields had been banned throughout the asteroid system.

"They're back at the ship," Sandy said. "Keeping guard." Suddenly, Sandy felt a little guilty for leaving her other dogs behind. They had always been faithful to her. "Want to come see them?" she asked.

Kella was in raptures over TJ and L2D2 as soon as she saw them. You'd think she'd never seen a robot before. But, then, Sandy had to remind herself that it wasn't so long ago that she'd made a compete fool of herself over Sparky. Now he was a chore.

"Why do you do it?" Sandy asked.

"Do what?" Kella asked, tracing the seams in TJ's head armor.

"Help your dad train dogs," Sandy said.

"It's fun," Kella said, absently. She was fingering the sensors and readouts clustered between TJ's ears. "These robots are so cool," Kella said. Her voice dripped with envy, but Sandy knew she was safe from Kella's jealousy turning to disdain. Kella would no more risk their temporary friendship than Sandy would.

Kella didn't want to be sent away from Sandy's spaceship full of robot dogs and other hi-tech toys. Sandy didn't want to be left alone without someone to talk to her. Another girl, her own age. Sandy knew the bargain they were tacitly making— she'd played it out on dozens of asteroids before. And she'd play it out on dozens of asteroids again.

So, Sandy made the most of her afternoon with Kella, wowing her with brainfeed videogames and gossiping. By the time Kella went home for dinner, Sandy had heard all about the Altarian boy Kella had a crush on (how could Kella *like* a boy with gelatinous skin? ugh), gotten some tips on training Sparky, and beaten Kella at *Space Stalkers* about a jillion times. It was a great afternoon, and Kella came over to repeat it almost every day until the Starstrongs had to leave. Again.

As always, it nearly broke Sandy's heart saying goodbye. When their spaceship took off, Sandy watched Kella's home grow smaller and smaller, through her bedroom window. Until it was just one asteroid in the rocky field of black space that was Sandy's home.

But then, she looked down at the fuzzy head resting on her knee, and Sandy realized she no longer felt quite as alone as before. All the time she'd spent with Kella, she'd spent with Sparky too.

And looking into Sparky's big brown eyes, Sandy found a comfort that couldn't be matched by LEDs. Sandy loved her robot dogs, but sometimes it seemed like all they were was expensive toys. Sparky might be a lot of trouble, but he was a *person*. A short, fuzzy person. But a person no less. (Hey, if beings who stick leftover scrap metal to their gelatinous skin to build ad hoc exoskeletons count as persons, Sparky *definitely* counted as a person.) Besides, now Sandy was the leader of an entire pack.

One girl, two robots, and one dog—out to conquer the asteroids.

11

THE PROMISE OF NEW HEFFE

The evacuation of Heffe VIII occurred when Jeaunia was only a pup. Her memories of waiting in the long lines on the hot spaceport tarmac were dim. She did remember playing games with her cousins on the crowded flight to Crossroads Station afterward, and she thought she could remember the view of the swollen Heffen sun through the spaceship's rear windows. She couldn't be sure, though. The bloody smear of red giant sunlight in her memories could have been a fabrication. She had been very young.

Jeaunia's entire body felt light when she saw the news flashing across the vid screens above the embassy offices—Expansionist Government Grants Deed for Type 1 Planet to the Confederacy of Heffen Refugees! Her paw pads rested firmly on the cool floor of Crossroads Station's refugee district, but she couldn't feel them anymore. Her people had lived in borrowed, rented corners of human space stations for Jeaunia's entire adult life. Finally, they would have a world of their own. A new world. With a young, yellow sun.

Jeaunia padded the rest of her way to work in a daze. She wrapped her arms tight around herself, as if she could hold on tight to the feeling inside: her people would have a planet again. Forests. Savannahs. Real homes.

The glass-paneled door to the daycare where Jeaunia worked required a key-badge to open. It kept the pups inside from getting out, and it kept unauthorized adults from getting in. Jeaunia looked through the glass of the door. The wriggly Heffen pups ran wild on the other side, and her co-worker Aga looked back at her. Aga waved and started speaking to Jeaunia before the door even finished sliding shut behind her.

"So..." Aga said. "Will you move there?" Her flop-tipped ears kept twitching on the top of her head, catching the sounds of pups rough-housing and playing throughout the room. It was hard to have a coherent conversation while working, but it made the workers crazy when they didn't even try.

"Well... yeah," Jeaunia said. She grabbed a smock to throw over her clothes and fur. It wouldn't entirely stop the pups from getting food and paint in the long fur of her white ruff and orange mane, but it would limit the damage.

Aga always had an easier time with the pups that way—her fur was short. She was ethnically Golan instead of Petriezski, meaning her muzzle was flatter and her fur much shorter than Jeaunia's. Apparently, back before the exodus of Heffe VIII, Golan had been underprivileged minorities. That hadn't remained true among the refugees on Crossroads Station. Losing their planet had been a great equalizer.

"Really?" Aga said, wrinkling her already flat nose. "You'll be... like a pioneer." A pup crawled on Aga's lap and grabbed one of her ears. "Living in the wilderness."

Jeaunia barked a laugh. "It won't be that bad," she said. "The government's been planning this for years. Since practically before we moved away from Heffe. I'm sure, they'll have the infrastructure in place in no time."

Aga nodded solemnly, considering that. Well, as solemnly as she could with the pup on her lap pulling her ears, mimicking her nod, and whining, "I want to paint, I want to paint" at her. Aga stood up and walked the pup over to an easel. "I've been following the news reports all day," she said. "Well, whenever I can."

Aga might have been following the reports all day, but Jeaunia had been listening to her family plan and scheme about their future lives on a hypothetical New Heffe for most of her life. Several of her littermates would probably join the building teams that would be the first to set out. She'd have to say goodbye to them soon.

"I still don't see what the big deal is," Aga said. "Trees? Land?" She shrugged. They'd had this argument before. Many times. Jeaunia had always kind of thought that if Aga hadn't known she was planning to move away to New Heffe some day, the Golan woman would have asked her out. As it was, there was no future for them together, so instead Aga just flirtingly teased her. "If you want trees, there's always the arboretum."

"Speaking of which..." Jeaunia tilted her head toward the corner of the nursery closest to the arboretum, wordlessly asking if they should take the pups there.

"Oh, right. But, no, we'll just go to the playground today. The arboretum's too hard on a day this busy." Aga looked around the room, tallying the pups up. "We're still four short. We'll go when they get here."

Jeaunia nodded, absently gathering up a few stray robo-toys the pups had left whirring away on the floor. She was standing in a small, enclosed room on a giant, rotating space station, surrounded by the vast emptiness of dark, black space. In her heart, however, she remembered a forest, green with trees and shrubs, ripe with juicy berries ready for the picking, and echoing with the happy shrieks of her littermates and cousins playing chase among the towering tree trunks.

How could she explain that? Aga had been a city pup before the exodus. Gleaming metal walls that partitioned off the limited domesticated patches of wilderness, keeping all the trees trapped inside tiny bubbles of arboretum—that was normal to her. Maybe Aga didn't belong on New Heffe. But Jeaunia's heart had been reaching ineffectually toward it—not knowing the exact shape or look of what it reached for, except that it would stand in for the world she'd lost—since she'd first set paw on Crossroads Station. What was the possibility of one romantic relationship compared to a whole homeworld?

"Yeah," Jeaunia said. "I'm definitely going." She placed a paw lightly on Aga's shoulder, twitching her claws just enough to catch her friends' attention. "Will you visit?"

Aga looked uncertain. Of course, her expression might have had more to do with trying to fend off a pup wielding a paintbrush full of chameleo-paint. "Interstellar flights are expensive..." she said. And relationships stretched across solar systems untenable.

Before Aga could say anything more, a harried Heffen mother showed up at the glass door, four pups clinging to her. One held each paw, another was clinging to her knees, and the final one had hold of her bushy tail. Jeaunia helped the woman divest herself of her litter. She was a nanny herself, so she'd be spending the day watching a different child. A privileged child in the human quarter. A single human child watched by a single Heffen nanny, as opposed to the entire roomful of bouncing Heffen pups, crowded together under the watchful but overworked eyes of Jeaunia and Aga.

As soon as the mother was gone, Aga handed around wristlets. The youngest pups needed help snapping them on, but the older litters were used to the routine. Within minutes, Jeaunia and Aga were out the sliding door and walking down the hallways of Crossroads Station with a whirlwind of pups skittering around them. The wristlets exerted a gentle electromagnetic force toward the master-wristlets Jeaunia and Aga wore, keeping the pups from straying far, but the entire walk was still an exercise in controlled chaos.

At the playground, Jeaunia adjusted the settings on her wristlet, expanding the field so the pups had the full run of the colorful jungle gyms and artificial gravity pockets. She sat down beside Aga on a bench at the perimeter of the wide, bubble-ceilinged room, and suddenly her pendant computer began to buzz. She flipped open the faux-locket case and looked at the messages streaming across the glowing screen, all of them from members of her big, messy family.

"What's wrong?" Aga asked.

Jeaunia's eyes must have betrayed her concern. "I'm not sure," she said, glancing rapidly between the locket screen and the gaggle of pups she was responsible for watching. The pups were more important—several of them looked like they would be whimpering for help with a particularly erratic grav-pocket momentarily—but the messages definitely had her worried.

Jeaunia shut the locket case and silenced the still-buzzing computer. "Some of my cousins are angry," she said. "Something about houses on New Heffe? I don't have time to read it now..."

As she spoke, both she and Aga saw one of the littlest pups get stuck in a gravity whirl. Aga ran to help him. Soon, Jeaunia found herself sucked into helping the pups in their play as well. The afternoon passed quickly and slowly at once. There was no time for anything but pups' concerns: who was playing the bouncy mount first; who pushed whom into the grav-pocket; who wanted to go home; and who missed their mums and dads.

Jeaunia was exhausted, as always, by the time she tightened the electro-magnetic field flowing from her wristlet. She watched the pups follow their wrists, reluctantly at first but more willingly as the pull grew stronger, toward her and Aga. She noticed something odd: there was a human, sitting on a bench at the far side of the park. A male with his arms crossed and his body leaned back. He looked harmless, but it was strange to see a human in the Heffen section of Crossroads Station, at least, one who wasn't buying food at one of the Golan booths. Spicy Golan confections had proved quite popular among the dominant species on Crossroads Station and was one of the main sources of Heffen income there.

After the playground, the pups were tired. Jeaunia and Aga put the littlest ones down for a nap, and the older ones read interactive stories on their own until snack time. Then they all played singing games together until, litter by litter, their parents came to pick them up.

All the while, Jeaunia worried over the messages in her locket. The pendant buzzed until she had to turn it off. When the final litter of pups were gone, she reopened the pendant computer. Messages streamed across the screen, all loading at once, all jumbled and out of order, too many and too fast to make sense.

"Your cousins are still angry?" Aga asked.

"I'd better get to my mom's quarters," Jeaunia said. "Besker is threatening never to speak to... someone? ...again. I think there's some sort of family meeting happening. Or maybe it already happened..."

Jeaunia looked helplessly at the mess of a nursery, robo-toys strewn everywhere, carpet covered in crumbs.

"Go on," Aga said. "I'll clean up. But you better make it up to me tomorrow."

Jeaunia swished her tail, dipped her ears, and said, "Thanks!" Then she was out the doors, rushing through the alleyways of merchant stands in the main ring of Crossroads Station toward the inner ring filled with individual living quarters. From the messages, she wasn't completely sure whether she should head to her mother's quarters or her aunt's... They were at different ends of the Heffen section, twenty minutes apart by tramavator. She decided to start with her mother's quarters. Those were close enough to walk to. If no one was there, she could still catch a tramavator car to Aunt Kally's.

Outside the door to her mother's quarters, Jeaunia heard muffled yelling. A male voice—probably her cousin Besker—and her mother's voice barked at each other. Reluctantly, Jeaunia reached her paw to the door and opened it. The yelling stopped. She peeked in.

Besker's long black fur was rumpled and wild. His eyes glared. He stood over Jeaunia's mother who sat in a chair, looking determinedly at a holo-painting of the old family estate hanging on the wall—blue-leafed trees surrounded a red-stone building. She was studiously avoiding Besker's glare.

"You're ruining all of our lives," Besker barked.

Jeaunia's mother hunched her shoulders a little more. Her ears were already flat. She still wouldn't look at him, and she didn't say anything.

Finally, Besker huffed and turned away from his aunt. He looked Jeaunia up and down before speaking to her. His tone was eerily different when he did, much softer. "We're having a big celebration in Ma's quarters. You're welcome to join us." He looked back at Jeaunia's mother, and his tone turned cold again: "You're not."

Besker stomped out of the quarters. The rumpled black fur of his mane and tail made him look like a storm cloud. A moment after the front door slammed behind Besker, another door opened. Jeaunia's littermate Bala peeked her muzzle out of their mother's bedroom and said, "He's gone?" She looked around to be sure and then came out. Her fur was a pale gold, and her mane much shorter than Besker's. "Thank heaven. He's such a brute. I won't miss him at all."

Bala continued talking about how much she'd always disliked Besker. Their mother continued staring at the holo-painting on the wall. The blue leaves in the painting shimmered, moving gently as if in a wind. Mother's shoulders began shaking, and Jeaunia realized that she was silently sobbing, tears matting the fur under her eyes.

Jeaunia's head was spinning. "What is going on?"

"It's my money," their mother said, still looking at the painting. Her gaze moved over the scene of trees and paths around the central red-stone building. She was actually looking at the painting now instead of merely staring at it. It seemed to give her strength. She turned to look at her daughters, half of her litter. "When you were newborn pups, my parents divided their estate. They gave the land and the home I'd grown up in to my sister. It broke my heart for them to give it away—I loved it so much. But I was alone with a litter to raise. I couldn't care for a place like that."

When Jeaunia and her littermates were pups, they'd lived in an apartment in the city. They'd visited their cousins on the family estate, but they hadn't lived there. Jeaunia remembered their apartment, but her heart had been at their cousins' home. She understood how her mother felt.

Her mother continued, "But I needed the money. They gave her the land; they gave me and Peff the equivalent money. Peff spent hers on buying another piece of land. I kept ours in the bank."

Jeaunia realized that she knew where this was going. "Wait, are you saying that you still have that money? Money equivalent to the value of the entire property that the family estate was on?" All kinds of emotions screamed inside Jeaunia's chest. But one question rang out above the others: "Why have we been so poor if you have that much money?!"

Her mother looked her steadily in the eye. Her ears stood tall. "It's Heffen money, Nia. It's no good on Crossroads Station."

"But it'll be worth a whole lot on New Heffe, I bet," Bala said. Her muzzle split into a grin, and her ears flicked.

"Yes," their mother said. She didn't look happy, just determined.

"That's why Besker's mad?" Jeaunia asked, still figuring it all out. "Does he... I mean..." She couldn't figure it out. "Why would that make him mad?"

Mother shrugged.

Bala said, "He wants the money."

That incited their mother to speak. "No, he wants his old life on Heffe VIII back. He doesn't see why anything should change."

Jeaunia could understand that. Even though it had been years ago, she still wanted that life back too. She'd been looking forward to reconstructing it on New Heffe. She wasn't sure why extra money in the family should be a problem. She wasn't sure why they weren't all celebrating at Aunt Kally's right now.

"But everything has changed," Mother continued. "And it's not my responsibility to coddle my sisters' grown-up pups. If Besker wants a large estate in a prime location on New Heffe, he can work for it. Just like I worked to care for you two and your brothers when I was younger. Now, I'm getting the reward." Mother's head tilted up, pointing her muzzle into the air. She looked proud. More than proud—haughty.

Jeaunia could see how Besker would find such an attitude hard to take. Her mother was always irritating when she got this way. "What do you mean, 'large estate in a prime location'?" Jeaunia asked.

Bala's brushy tail began swishing wildly behind her, and their mother got up. She went over to the computer console and called up a rotating hologram of New Heffe—blue oceans and gold continents, frosted with white swirls of cloud—in place of the painting of the old family estate on Heffe VIII. It was the same image Jeaunia had seen on every holo-screen today.

Mother zoomed the image in, and one of the gold continents grew and expanded until it took over the entire scene. As the golden continent grew closer, blue snakes of river appeared. Greener and ruddier patches appeared. The gold took on the mottled texture of forests seen from above. Angular gray shapes appeared amidst the trees. Finally, the image was magnified enough to see that the angular gray shapes were streets and buildings. Whole networks of cities.

"Is this from a photograph?" Jeaunia asked. "They can't have built these cities already."

"This is an artists' rendition," Mother said. "But it's from blueprints that have been under development for years." She sounded really excited. She held out a paw and pointed a single dull claw at a corner of the hologram. "That's my estate."

Jeaunia peered at the angular splotch of gray surrounded by blotchy gold. It was near a spider's web of gray intersections. But not too near. It looked like it was a comfortable distance from a very big city.

It didn't look anything like the memory of space and air beneath the branches of the trees on Old Heffe that Jeaunia carried inside her heart. But, then, a zoomed out artists' rendition of her old home might not look much like home to Jeaunia either. She tried to feel excited. She mostly felt confused and conflicted. "You've already picked where to live? Isn't that what everyone else is doing at Aunt Kally's right now?"

Mother shrugged again, nose still held high.

"Aren't we all going to live near each other?" Jeaunia asked.

"I can't help what choices others make," Mother said. She turned the hologram off. The screen went dark. No rendition of New Heffe; no painting of Heffe VIII.

Jeaunia stared at the dark screen, trying not to feel the same blank darkness inside. This wasn't going how she'd expected. Or how she'd planned.

"Mom's giving me an advance on my inheritance," Bala said. "So, Mekal and I are going to buy a place in the city near her estate. That way we can take our pups out to visit all the time. Like we used to visit Aunt Kally's when we were pups."

"I'd give you an advance as well, Nia," Mother said, tilting her head to the side, looking at her daughter closely. "I'm giving advances to both of your brothers and their families. Or, since you're still alone, you could live with me, help me care for my estate. I'd pay you."

The holo-screen was still dark, but Jeaunia pointed to where the spider's web of city lines had been. "Would I need an advance to afford to live in that city?"

"The capital?" Mother asked. "Probably."

Now it all made sense. Jeaunia didn't feel dark inside anymore. Just cold. "What about Aunt Kally and our cousins? Where will they live?"

"Wherever they want," Mother said. Then she revised her statement, "Wherever they can afford. They're welcome to visit." Suddenly, she looked small and sad. She looked away from Jeaunia. "Somehow, I don't think they'll want to."

The coldness in Jeaunia's chest clenched and tightened. She felt angry with her mother but also angry at her aunt and cousins. They should all be discussing this together. They should all be celebrating! Jeaunia clenched her paw into a fist and slammed it into the wall beside the dark, empty holo-screen.

Bala's muzzle gaped open. She stared at Jeaunia, stunned. "What's wrong with you? You just found out that you're rich, and we have a new world to live on. My pups don't have to grow up on this station. They'll get to run free in Mother's estate. You can even live on her estate. We're all better off than we were this morning."

"Not all of us," Jeaunia muttered, turning away. She stomped to the door, claws clicking angrily against the floor. "I'm going to Aunt Kally's," she shouted without turning back to look at them. She flattened her ears, refusing to listen to anything her mother or sister said as she stormed through the door.

Except Jeaunia didn't go to Aunt Kally's. She walked to the tramavator, even waited for a tram car to come. But she didn't take it. She watched the tram car fill with other Heffens and a few avian and reptilian aliens, but she didn't get on. She watched the doors slide shut, and the tram car pulled away.

Jeaunia walked the corridors of the station, seeing the shadow of her orange-furred body reflected dully in the metal walls. Her blurry reflection followed her as she wandered aimlessly, unwilling to go back to her mother and sister; yet unable to go be with her aunt and cousins instead.

She knew that if she went to be with her cousins, she'd get swept away in their plans. They were surely voting and negotiating and arguing over where to buy homesteads on New Heffe. Except it wouldn't be near the homesteads of her own mother and litter. She didn't want to choose which part of her family to be near. She liked it here—everyone was close. Why did that have to change?

But then she imagined trees and open air instead of metal corridors, closing her in. To hell with them all! Jeaunia wished that the swollen red giant of a sun that had scorched Aunt Kally's land had burned her mother's money as well.

She hadn't been rich this morning; she didn't want to be rich now. She wanted to be surrounded by her family. But she didn't want to hear Besker say that Mother should split the money between them all, that Mother was being selfish, that Mother was ruining the family. And she knew he'd say those things. Aunt Kally would agree, and her other cousins too.

They were the ones being selfish. It was Mother's money. Except why wouldn't Mother just give it to them? Money was nothing next to family.

Except... Why should she have to?

Did they all value money more than each other?

Jeaunia's wandering paws brought her back to the playground where she and Aga had brought the nursery pups earlier. She sat on the same bench where her locket computer had buzzed incessantly at her all afternoon, and she stared at the empty play equipment—brightly colored climbing structures and shimmers in the air, giving the tell-tale sign of grav-fluctuations.

The empty playground made her think of Old Heffe. The planet was still there, baked and broiled by a swollen sun. No one on it.

After a while, Jeaunia noticed that the human man was still sitting on the far side of the playground, staring at the empty equipment much as she had been. When he noticed her staring at him, he smiled, a weak turn of his primate lips. He looked sad and tired, like she felt. Jeaunia smiled back, and the human man gestured at the space on the bench beside him, inviting her to come over and sit beside him.

Jeaunia's ears flicked back, uncertain, but then the human man shrugged in such an unguarded, innocuous way that she decided she could use the company. Her tail swished behind her as she crossed the playground to sit beside him. When she sat with a comfortable amount of empty space between them, her tail curled around her side primly.

"What do you think of the images of New Heffe?" the human man asked.

Jeaunia narrowed her eyes at the human, trying to figure out why he cared. "It's beautiful," she said.

He nodded, but his lower lip pouted out. He still didn't look happy. "I lived on Heffe for, oh, about seven or eight years," he said. Then he looked at her, like he was sizing her up. "You must have been a puppy when..."

"Yes," she agreed. Neither of them wanted to refer directly to the evacuation of Heffe VIII. "I guess you lived there about as long as I did." She laughed at the realization. "What do you think? Does it look as beautiful as the Heffe you remember?"

Together, they stared at the image of a blue, gold, and green world, slowly turning on the vid screens.

"No," he said. "But memory does funny things to a place. Makes it glow."

Jeaunia turned her gaze back to the human man and tilted her head to the side. He looked old; he had the wrinkles on his face that naked-skinned species got when they aged. His head fur was thin, wispy, and gray. He'd have been an adult when he lived on Heffe. He'd seen it through an adult's eyes. "What brought you to Heffe VIII?" she asked. "My understanding is that there weren't a lot of out-worlders who lived there..." It was strange to talk to an alien man who might know as much—or more—about her homeworld as she did. And he had the knowledge from a different angle than all the stories she'd heard from her mother and aunt.

The human frowned now and titled his head down, like he didn't want to answer the question. Eventually, he reluctantly said, "I was a solar physicist at Wespirtech, young and arrogant. The Petriezski government hired me as a consultant."

Jeaunia looked away from the human. Tears threatened to well up in her eyes. She looked upward and held her eyes wide, trying to stop them. But she couldn't stop her ears from flattening atop her head. "You're one of the scientists who accelerated the sun's expansion."

"I was part of the team, yes." He stuck a hand out. "My name's Alan."

Jeaunia didn't take the human's hand in her paw, and he let it fall back into his lap. She intended to glare at him. He shouldn't take his role in the past so lightly. He shouldn't dodge his responsibility for how things had unfolded. Their sun, a red giant, had been dying, but they'd have had another hundred years or so. Or maybe it was a thousand? Jeaunia wasn't actually sure. She hadn't studied the science. But she knew their sun's death had been slow, and after the Wespirtech scientists had tried their experiments, the expansion happened much faster.

Yet, as she watched the human's face, she could see he wasn't dodging responsibility. He was simply having a conversation, years after the fact. A conversation that he didn't have to have. Honestly, she was surprised he still cared about Heffe at all. Still, she couldn't stop herself from asking, "Have you blown any other suns up since then?"

"I don't do physics anymore," the human said. "I stopped after... that."

Jeaunia nodded curtly, but she kept sitting beside Alan.

"I was trying to help..." Alan said weakly. "It wasn't supposed to..."

"I don't care," Jeaunia cut him off. She didn't want to listen to his guilt. Still, it intrigued her that he looked so consumed by it. The more she thought about it, she realized she'd seen Alan around the Heffen sections of Crossroads Station before, buying Golan food, attending plays put on by the Heffen Actors' Guild, and watching the pups on the playgrounds.

"Are you planning to go to New Heffe?" she asked him suddenly.

"Oh, no, no," Alan said, clearly uncomfortable with the question. He probably thought he wouldn't be welcome there. And he might not be. Even so, Jeaunia wasn't sure how welcome he felt here.

"Are you sure?" she asked. "I feel like I've seen you around the Heffen parts of the station a lot."

Alan didn't have anything to say to that, and their conversation awkwardly petered out. Eventually, he excused himself and hurried away from the playground, heading in the direction of the more human parts of the station.

Jeaunia watched him go, and she wondered how old he'd

been when he came to Heffe VIII as an arrogant, young scientist. Possibly the age that she was now. And yet, his life seemed to be as consumed by the destruction of her homeworld—her species' cradle in the universe and her own personal childhood—as her own life.

Jeaunia's pendant computer buzzed again, and she opened the locket to see more messages from her cousins. "Where are you?" "Are you coming?" "We don't want to start making choices without you..." Except, of course, they would.

And they should.

"Go ahead," Jeaunia messaged back. "I'll be there shortly, but you don't have to wait."

In response, she was barraged with messages asking, "Are you sure???" But she'd already told them what to expect from her.

Jeaunia took her time strolling through the metal corridors of Crossroads Station. By the time she arrived Aunt Kally's quarters, the small front room was packed full of her relatives—everyone except her own mother and sister—and they were all arguing heatedly, passionately, but civilly about several different cities planned for the northern end of one of the gold-green continents of New Heffe. One was closer to an ocean. Another was cheaper. Yet a third sounded like it was likely to have a powerful art scene—many actors, musicians, and writers were already planning to buy lots there.

Jeaunia sat cross-legged on the floor, like one of the pups she'd watched all afternoon, and listened to the animated arguments rage back and forth. These were the people who'd be on New Heffe—adults with their own lives, not the young cousins she remembered playing with among the trees.

One of her cousin's pups, a boy named Ojo, came peeking out from Aunt Kally's bedroom where the rest of his litter was probably playing games. He scurried into the middle of the room and crawled into Jeaunia's lap.

The little boy turned his muzzle up close enough that she could feel the breath from his nose on her ear. He whispered, "Are we really all leaving? This is my home. I don't want to leave Crossroads Station."

Jeaunia squeezed Ojo around his fuzzy middle. "Don't you want a new home? Don't you want to live surrounded by trees and grassy plains? With a big blue sky above you?" she whispered back.

Ojo shook his head fiercely. "There are trees in the arboretum. And I don't want some stupid blue sky blocking out the stars. Or for the gravity to be the same everywhere. So boring!"

Jeaunia wanted to laugh, but instead she nodded solemnly. This was where he'd grown up. For Ojo, leaving Crossroads Station because his parents decided to move away wasn't all that different from when she'd had to leave Old Heffe.

"Tell you what," she whispered back. "What if I stay here, and you can come visit me when you're older?"

Ojo didn't answer right away, and Jeaunia realized the room had fallen silent around them. All of her cousins and her Aunt Kally were watching her. They'd heard what she'd said to the pup.

Besker asked, "You're not moving to New Heffe?"

Jeaunia tried to speak, but all her words got tangled up. She hadn't really thought this through yet, but she already had a whole room full of family looking at her expectantly, waiting for her to sort her life out to their liking. It might not be so bad to have some distance from them. Her friend Aga had been telling her that for years, but she'd been too afraid to listen. This was her family.

"Of course she's moving to New Heffe," Aunt Kally said to all the others. Her tone superior. "She's just trying to make Ojo feel better."

The presumptuousness of Aunt Kally's statement made Jeaunia angry, but she felt too tired to argue. She didn't want to explain herself or her uncertainty to everyone here. None of them would understand—they were worried about big things like where to raise their pups and long-standing feuds over inheritances. Jeaunia didn't want to pick sides. She simply wanted to spend time with all of them.

But that wasn't going to happen—here or on New Heffe. They'd all been too busy for her for a long time now.

She thought about Alan, still consumed by a disaster that had happened to someone else's world, trapped in the past. She didn't want her life to be defined by a disaster in the past. And truly, it hadn't been. She was happy here. The promise of New Heffe had always been tantalizing, but it hadn't stopped her from enjoying her life. It hadn't stopped her from spending time with Aga while they worked.

Then she thought about Ojo—and all the pups she watched at the daycare with Aga every day—and how they'd never lived on a planet. Only here. On Crossroads Station. To them, a space station was enough. It was home. And it was beautiful.

Maybe Jeaunia hadn't been looking forward to the promise of a new world so much as she'd been looking back, missing her childhood. But her childhood was over, and a new planet wouldn't bring it back. A new planet wouldn't make her cousins young again; wouldn't erase their arguments and differing priorities; wouldn't make life easy.

"I can't make you and Mama get along with each other," Jeaunia told her aunt. "And I can't make her give you her money. But I do know that I don't want to be in the middle of it. I have a life here. Maybe when you're all settled, I'll come visit. Maybe I'll even want to stay. But for now? No, I'm not moving to New Heffe. And maybe not ever."

Jeaunia gave Ojo another squeeze and then eased him off of her lap. She left Aunt Kally's quarters before any of them could figure out what to say.

Jeaunia walked back through the halls of Crossroads Station to her own quarters. Her quarters might not be filled with trees or surrounded by grasslands. But they were her own small rooms, filled with the pieces of her own life. And she was looking forward to waking up in the morning and telling Aga she was going to stay. They hadn't talked about it earlier, because Jeaunia knew it would have been too hard. Maybe tomorrow, Jeaunia would finally ask her out. Maybe she'd take her some flowers, too.

And maybe when Jeaunia did go visit her family on New Heffe, Aga would come along, and they could visit their people's new homeworld together. For now, though, it was time to get serious about her life on Crossroads Station, instead of waiting for an imaginary future.

12

___

HARVESTING WISHES

Most genies offer three. Where do they get them? The Harvester is an old woman, who wears a four-leafed clover in her locket and a garland of dandelions on her hair. The locket was a gift from a suitor, many years before, bought at the Crossroads Station bazaar. The dandelions have to be supplied fresh, daily. So, she keeps a greenhouse in the aft of her ship. The Harvester tells her genie customers that the wishes she harvests come from the overripe gold flowers gone to fluffy white seed. This, of course, is not true, but the genies love it.

Occasionally, a particularly sneaky genie will "pocket" a sample of the dandelions, hoping to grow a harvest of his own. But, the Harvester altered the dandelion DNA long ago, and the flowers will only grow in a soil laced with her secret mix of protein supplements.

The most ingenious genie that the Harvester ever encountered tried to track down the original planetary source of dandelions. He reasoned it must be a magical world full of happiness, rainbows, and joy. Unfortunately, the founders of New Earth erased all traces of the original Earth's location during a nasty legal battle with Earth IX. Neither planet won exclusive rights to "Paris" or "Rome;" New Earth won the rights to "New York." The genie won nothing and skulked his way back to the Harvester to buy a year's supply of wishes, packaged in bundles of three.

So, where do the wishes come from? The Harvester disables her shipboard navigation systems every time she begins the trip. So, in the strictest sense, even she does not know. But she can find her way. At the bluish star, she taps the thrusters twice. When there's the triangle of pinkish stars, she hangs a hard right. Then, right at the edge of the dust cloud, where the icy specks merely tickle the hull of her ship, the Harvester turns the hyper engines on full. She doesn't watch the ship clock or count the seconds. When enough time has passed, the Harvester just knows, and she brings the ship to a full stop.

Outside, the space is clear. Her path brings the Harvester to the nadir of an orbit perpendicular to the plane of asteroids orbiting her own, secret, deathly silent black hole. An extra second on the hyper drive and her ship would be too close, but the Harvester never gets it wrong.

From her vantage point, the Harvester scans the rings of asteroids, but she almost always finds what she's looking for by the naked eye. So, with her graying tresses mirrored, shadowy in the glass, the Harvester looks past her reflection and watches the asteroids through the ship windows. Together they circle the black hole, swirling toward it, until they disappear. Except for one. She'll spot one, and, then, after watching long enough, she'll spot another.

Individual asteroids following their own, bizarre gravitational rules. Ignoring the pull of the black hole.

The Harvester notes these aberrations down, and when she's found enough of them... She harvests. Inside each aberrant asteroid, sometimes a canker on its surface and sometimes a heart in its very core, a geode of hypercrystals resides. The

Harvester chips them off or cracks the asteroid wide, freeing the hidden crystals.

The crystals, when she finds them, are coupled to complimentary geodes in complimentary asteroids orbiting entirely different gravitational wells in entirely different, alternate universes. The asteroids, while reigned by their geodes, follow these alternate gravity paths, creating their telltale, seemingly illogical orbits. Why so many there? Mixed into the field of asteroids around that black hole? The Harvester doesn't know, but a hyperstar exploded there. Back when the black hole began.

The Harvester breaks the geodes open, shattering the crystalline pattern, and decoupling the hypercrystals. They sparkle, each tiny crystal feeling and dallying with the pull of hypercrystals in alternate universes fanning across potentiality.

The rest of the process is easy. A milli-mole of hypercrystal, soldered to a positronic picochip encased in a language processing micro-computer... The Harvester packages them in hand sewn pouches, made from Antarian arachnid silicon-silk. In threes, the wishes clack inside their pouches, each tiny computer housed in a pleasing, cheerfully colored aluminum shell. They look like marbles.

The Harvester discovered her wish farm eons ago. She'd been harboring a genetic errant on her ship. His crime was old, and he'd hid from it so long, changing his mind and body so many times, that the Harvester felt he could no longer be held responsible. The azure-skinned, Buddha-bellied alien with the deep laugh who she knew was hardly the wispy green Anili-idaen who had eaten his own mother anymore. Most of his memories from that time had been erased by the constant genetic phasing, and she knew he would never dare commit any crime—other than running—again.

Nonetheless, the errant and his booming laugh, after weeks in the asteroids, drove the Harvester nearly crazy. She stopped tending her shipboard garden, which came up all weeds in her neglect, and turned to the out of doors. Out of the ship.

The Harvester floated, peaceful and serene, in her spacesuit. She kept herself tethered to the now loathsome ship and its unwanted tenant but otherwise bounded lightly from one hanging asteroid to another. As her suited hand brushed one of the rocky surfaces, a dome of brittle rock crumbled at her touch, revealing the sparkling hollow of crystals beneath. Thinking the crystals pretty, the Harvester chipped them out of their cranny in the asteroid, stored them in a pocket of her spacesuit, and brought them back with her.

The rest is history. Or fable, according to the authorities at Crossroads Station, but everyone suspects the Harvester paid them to play it that way.

While shining the crystals, buffing them with a sonic-razor, the Harvester noticed they looked awfully similar to the crystalline nodes in an elasti-particle wired compu-chip the errant was fiddling with. He'd been trying to upgrade her shipboard computers with worse than mixed success. The Harvester asked the errant if she could have one of the burned out boards and tried wiring one of her shiny new crystals into the place of the fizzled node. It was delicate, tricky work, and the errant, in his overbearing way, hovered over her. Heckling.

"I wish you'd leave me alone," she muttered and felt the strangest spark of electrical activity under her fingers. Then, even stranger, though the errant leaned closer and boomed at her about how she'd fried the crystal and needed to be more careful, the Harvester felt his presence back away, move across the room, and leave her alone. Exactly as she'd wished. It was a duality of moment, as if she were living in one universe and simultaneously hallucinating the reality of another.

But the moment ended, and the errant was still hovering. His pudgy girth bumped her, jostling her arm as the Harvester inserted a new asteroid crystal. This time she exclaimed, "I wish you'd go away and turn yourself in!"

The duality happened again. In reality, the errant laughed a deep, jovial, bubbling laugh. But in her hallucination, he was taken aback. His eyes turned down, and after a moment of serious thought, the errant said, "You're right. I should pay for my crime." After a long sigh, "I can never live peacefully with it hanging over my head..."

But then the duality faded.

The intensity of the experience did not.

"Hell," the Harvester exclaimed, "I've burnt out another crystal."

When the Harvester finally got the next crystal wired, she was careful not to make any wishes. Unlike the others, the third crystal didn't burn out, blackening with fine crack lines. No, it sparkled finely in the compu-chip, and the Harvester inserted it into the hardware of a palm computer. A smooth, egg-shaped device with voice recognition and the most powerful actuator chip she could find.

That was the first fully manufactured wish.

Over the years, the Harvester fiddled with the specs until she got them down from egg-sized to marble-sized, using the weakest actuator chip that could actually couple universes, producing results instead of mere hallucinations.

She sold them, but she never tried one herself, except to test them. Those wishes were always simple—"I wish my wilted dandelion were fresh again"—nothing that mattered.

And then her suitor returned. He told her he wanted to buy wishes, and the Harvester told him she didn't deal with customers. Only genies.

"I'm a genie," he said. "Sell me the usual package. That's three, right?"

"Multiples of three," she answered, thinking she should get back to her ship and out of the crowded Crossroads Station bazaar. Unconsciously, she fingered the four leaf clover pendant at her neck.

"One multiple will do."

"You're not a genie," she said. "Your phenotype is exactly the same as it's always been."

He refrained from answering cheekily with something like, "You mean I'm still handsome?" But he could see her eyes measuring him. Liking what she saw. As she always had.

"Besides, you haven't committed any crimes to run away from," she added, dropping the pendant suddenly. It fell back against her throat.

"I'm the old kind of genie," he said. "You've got me trapped in a bottle."

"You mean a lamp."

"Let me out," he said.

"I don't sell wishes," she said. "Find a real genie and threaten to turn him in. There's your wish."

But her suitor followed her through the bazaar. As she neared her ship, she was skipping, running through the crowd. Her dandelions fell out of her hair. But her suitor kept her in sight nonetheless.

He gathered the fallen dandelions, one by one, into a droopy bouquet. He stood at the edge of her airlock, bouquet in hand. It could have been twenty years ago, when he had last pursued her. When she was newly the Harvester. A young Harvester.

Seeing her suitor there, feeling that loopy sense of time folding back on itself, being reminded of her younger self... She couldn't help but let him in. For old time's sake. For the younger self that was gone, subsumed inside an older woman.

Another choice. Another life... Surely, there was a universe out there, across the multitudinous massless masses, where a young Harvester and a young suitor...

No, she would give her suitor no wishes. Nor would she make wishes for him.

The Harvester and the suitor sat together. They drank tea. They talked. It was quiet, and the Harvester didn't feel she had recaptured her lost youth. Only looked at it from a new angle.

"Give me another chance," her suitor said. He put his hands out, old and worn. And the Harvester, with only a slight hesitation, took them.

It was the same universe it had always been. But completely different. And the Harvester wouldn't have had it any other way.

ABOUT THE AUTHOR

Mary E. Lowd is a prolific science-fiction and furry writer in Oregon. She's had more than 200 short stories and a dozen novels published, always with more on the way. Her work has won three Ursa Major Awards, ten Leo Literary Awards, and four Cóyotl Awards. She edited FurPlanet's ROAR anthology series for five years, and she is now the editor and founder of the furry e-zine *Zooscape*. She lives in a crashed spaceship, disguised as a house and hidden behind a rose garden, with an extensive menagerie of animals, some real and some imaginary.

For more information:
marylowd.com

To read Mary's short stories:
deepskyanchor.com

ALSO BY MARY E. LOWD

Otters in Space

Otters In Space

Otters In Space 2: Jupiter, Deadly

Otters In Space 3: Octopus Ascending

The Celestial Fragments (A Labyrinth of Souls Trilogy)

The Snake's Song

The Bee's Waltz

The Otter's Wings

The Entangled Universe

Entanglement Bound

The Entropy Fountain

Starwhal in Flight

Xeno-Spectre

Hell Moon

The Ancient Egg

In a Dog's World

Jove Deadly's Lunar Detective Agency

The Necromouser and Other Magical Cats

You're Cordially Invited to Crossroads Station

Queen Hazel and Beloved Beverly

Tri-Galactic Trek

Nexus Nine

Some Words Burn Brightly: An Illuminated Collection of Poetry